D0772502

Season in Purgatory

Season in Purgatory

Thomas Keneally

COLLINS
London - Sydney
1976

William Collins Sons & Co Ltd
London · Glasgow · Sydney · Auckland
Toronto · Johannesburg

First published 1976
© Thomas Keneally 1976
ISBN 0 00 222471 2
Set in Monotype Baskerville
Made and Printed in Great Britain by
William Collins Sons & Co Ltd Glasgow

Contents

to my brother
John Patrick

AUTHOR'S NOTE. This mere narrative derives from real events that occurred off the Dalmatian coast in 1943 and 1944. However, the characters – with the exception of Tito himself – are entirely fictional and are not meant to refer, either as regards appearance, behaviour or career, to any officer, doctor or partisan who occupied that place and period.

A few months ago the spirited Yugoslav widow Mrs Moja Javich visited her son, a wine importer, in London. She had the son invite to dinner at his Fulham villa her dearest friend, David Pelham, thirteen years her junior.

These days Pelham was one of the best orthopaedic surgeons in the western world. He had written the standard works on compound fracture and hip-socket injury. But he was not a characteristic great surgeon. Once he had refused a knighthood because he thought such things vain and archaic, but then was vain enough to let his secret rejection become known throughout his profession.

She knew something of his personal life too. He had had no children by his only wife, who died of cancer in 1964. Now he lived with a lean and beautiful Knightsbridge lady and seemed to be happy. But out of some sensitivity for the past he did not bring her with him to his meeting with the Yugoslav widow. He came alone.

He was shocked to find how tired Mrs Javich seemed. All the fine lines of her face were blurred. Though some of his old passion for her recurred he could not permit himself to caress her firmly, because of his *real* fear that her frame would not stand it. She had pain in her chest . . . a virus, she said. Pelham looked at her throat and got some Librium for her from an all-night chemist. But at the end of the second course, when the

7

pain and breathlessness made her hang her head over her plate, he called the ambulance.

'Don't you dare, David,' she panted, even as he dialled the number.

In St Stephen's they began treating her for coronary occlusion. When Pelham was let in to see her and beheld the anonymous and thick-grained robe the hospital had put her in, it struck him that she looked as if dressed for her funeral already. This presentiment was all the more astounding since, as a working surgeon, he was used to dealing daily with people robed in this way.

He said, 'You rest well, Moja.' On the way out he felt the urge to stop nurses and junior medical staff and tell them, 'Please take care of that old woman. She is a Balkan goddess and kept me alive on the terrible island of Mus.'

He returned to St Stephen's early the next afternoon, after finishing his own operating list at the Royal Free Hospital. He met young Javich in the foyer and knew at once that Moja was gone.

'Just now,' said young Javich. It seemed to Pelham that the young man was doubly bereft. In his home-country the neighbour women would dress his mother in veil and ceremonial apron and wail around her body. And the men would solemnly drink with him in the same room as dear dead Moja. Here, in London, he would receive only the pallid comfort of white condolence cards, and business associates would sometimes squeeze his shoulder.

Pelham thought, we believed ourselves so clever not to leave our brains or viscera on the savage island of Mus. Now Moja's escape was terminated.

He rang the Superintendent and was allowed to see Moja. She looked very thin, her face transparent. The saline equipment stood idle by her bed and he could see the little hole in her hand where the anti-coagulant needle had gone.

Downstairs, he took Javich by the arm. There would be time for a double Scotch.

Javich said, 'The funeral will be Thursday.'

'Thursday? But . . .'

'She doesn't mind being buried in England. I'm in England. You're in England.'

Pelham thought of the miserable cemeteries of the London boroughs.

Javich said, 'It'll be the graveyard of the Serbian Orthodox Church in Bethnal Green. It's a little corner of Serbia.'

'In Tower Hamlets?'

'Yes. Truly, she would have liked it.'

Over their whisky Javich startled Pelham.

'You were one of her great loves.'

Pelham coughed. 'I didn't know whether she ever told you . . . about our . . .'

'Not in any way that would debase it.'

'No. Good.' Without warning, there in the saloon of The Victory, Pelham was forced to excuse himself and go to weep in the Gents.

On Thursday morning, Moja Javich, beloved of Javich and Pelham and at one time matriarch of the Twenty Second Partisan Division was put into the earth in a sunny corner of the graveyard of her people's church in Bethnal Green. The place, well walled off from traffic, louts and schoolchildren, suited her better than Pelham could have hoped.

Also present at the funeral were Fielding (who had handed Pelham instruments on Mus and was now a Professor of Slavonic Studies at Hull University) and his Slovene wife Jela.

The death left Pelham a duty to fulfil. A month ago he flew to Belgrade and, hiring a car, drove south amongst the hills of lower Serbia to a village close to Čačak. Here an old man called Jovan, once an orderly of his on the island of Mus, ran a stone-cutting business. Or rather, sat in the sun, squinting and whimsical, with a white wool skullcap on his head, while his sons ran it for him.

Jovan gave Pelham a high-pitched fluting welcome, summoned his sons, poured slivovitz – whose taste is the taste of high danger and of youth to Pelham – and produced those syrupy sweetmeats called *slatko*. Then they spoke.

'Jovan,' said Pelham, 'I want you to cast me a wayside memorial stone for Moja. In the true Serbian manner. I think something such as: I am Moja Javich, matron and mentor of the Twenty-Second Partisan Division in the island of Mus and later of Fourth Partisan Division in the mountains of Bosnia. Saviour of many wounded, I could not save myself and succumbed on . . . and then you put the date, Jovan.'

'You have the style of wayside stones exactly, comrade doctor.'

'Thank you, Jovan.'

'What design should the stone be, friend?'

'You know, Jovan. The instruments she used. And do you think . . .?'

'What?'

'Do you think you could engrave that X-ray machine?'

'Yes. We can do that. In the primitive manner.'

'The only manner to do it.'

'One problem. There are restrictions on *krajputashi* now. You would have to get a licence from the Monuments Undersecretary of the Council in Čačak.'

'My God!'

'I know the man. He isn't a bad fellow. We could go and see him now if you like.'

Then they drove the few miles to Čačak, past its Teutonic cathedral, and halted the car in front of a two-storey building surmounted by a neon star to cheer and shine on Serbians in the night. The Undersecretary's office was no more than six feet square. The Undersecretary was intense and balding, with the unpleasant manners of a man most likely made for better things than decreeing who was or was not ideologically fit to raise a *krajputashi* at the side of the highway.

Jovan told the man that he and the renowned comrade Doctor Pelham were seeking leave to raise a memorial stone to Moja Javich who had grown up in Čačak.

Pelham could not understand everything that was said. The Undersecretary's accent was strange and Pelham, having learned his Serbo-Croat under stress on Mus, had forgotten much of it The conversation, however, went on these lines –

Undersecretary: Grew up in Čačak? I believe she went to school in Vienna. And to Vienna University after that.

Jovan: But her family were Čačak people.

Undersecretary: Gentry! You and I lived in their shadow, Jovan.

Jovan: She became a partisan. You have no idea . . .

Undersecretary: We were all partisans.

Jovan: She was a '41 partisan. What vintage were you?

Undersecretary: I'm not seeking a *krajputashi* for myself.

To Pelham this talk was intolerable. He interrupted. 'For God's sake! Big Josip knew her . . .'

'Big Josip? *Tito?*'

'She gave him charcoal tablets for nausea.'

'Nausea?' The Undersecretary seemed uneasy to have the demi-god's symptoms dumped in his lap.

'She gave him suppositories,' said Pelham. 'He sent her son a telegram on her death.'

Jovan said, signifying love by the motions of his hand, 'There was even talk that they were . . .' He remembered though that Pelham had also been close to Moja, and now became embarrassed for his sake.

The English surgeon said, 'It is quite likely that Tito would demand a *krajputashi* for her himself. He has probably not thought of it because he is a Croat and Croats don't go in for wayside monuments, but if I were to telephone him, he'd want it then.'

Jovan said resoundingly, 'It's the truth.'

And the Undersecretary could tell it was. You could see him think, what will I gain in any case by being too finicking?

Dropping Jovan at his shop door after the interview, Pelham said he would be back in August to see the monument.

Jovan said, 'Why don't we both go over to Mus as well, my doctor?'

Pelham flinched. Mus had such strange connotations for him. Not only the place of youth, but, as well, the place of blood sacrifice and wine, of love and the smell of gangrene. Above all, of near madness.

Jovan said, 'It's an island for very rich tourists now. They bathe naked in Gievisa. Soon the travel agencies will find it. It will be too late then to make a pilgrimage.'

Pelham looked full into Jovan's squinty eyes. 'I don't know, friend. My mind's a little full of Moja now.'

He thought in self-disgust: even in Serbo-Croat, that's all I'm willing to say of her.

Chapter 1 Twinkum's Villa

At the end of September 1943, David Pelham was working as a junior medical officer in a military hospital in Bari. He was then a tall dark-eyed man of 27. He had come up the Italian coast with a parachute division of the Eighth Army. The hospital was situated in a girls' school. For perhaps a week he had acted as anaesthetist for more senior medical officers who were at work on thoracic or abdominal battle wounds. Sometimes he was permitted to operate on minor shrapnel wounds himself and, in one particular rush hour, to amputate a mashed and shattered leg. But very quickly the fighting moved northwards. Pelham's unit became a base hospital. Within a fortnight brigadiers were coming in to have their piles done and their veins repaired. The beds which yesterday had been full of pathetically wounded, of the grey faces of those who would never grow old, now went to rowdy gonorrhoea cases from the Sicily campaign.

Some weeks before he had signed his name to a form that asked for volunteer medical officers with parachute training to perform battle surgery under primitive conditions. He had signed it wistfully expecting no result. But he reasoned that if one were to serve in the Medical Corps, one should seek to perform war surgery. Otherwise he might as well have become a general practitioner in the North Wales of his ancestors.

One day he decided to telephone all those senior officers

who had known his father. He found himself talking to a brigadier.

'Pelham? Is your father George Pelham?'

'Yes.'

'The orthopod?'

'Yes, sir.'

'I say! And what is it? You feel you're made for better things than tinkering round a base hospital?'

'I want to get surgical experience, sir.'

'Fair enough. We could get you sent to a forward receiving station. Up to the Gustav line, eh?'

'Very grateful, sir.'

'Not too quick. First I'll find out about this other thing you put your name to.'

'A lot of trouble for you, sir.'

'Need I say? Your father's been very kind to me.'

The next evening Pelham sat in the bar of the Imperiale with a black-haired nurse from the base hospital. Pelham was an Anglo-Catholic. He practised his religion to the extent of never fornicating with a woman just because she was available. This woman was available and a bore. Already she had used fifteen minutes explaining to him how potent cliques in the Littlehampton Lawn Tennis Association had worked eighteen months to corner her father into resigning his presidency. Daddy had never been worth much since that day, she told Pelham.

At the stage when an accountant called Gollings was crucially betraying Daddy in the changing room, a brigadier appeared at the nurse's shoulder.

'I say, it's you,' said the brigadier. It was the man Pelham had appealed to the day before. 'I recognized the strong features,' he said.

Pelham introduced him to the nurse. Oh, he knew Littlehampton, used often to sail round Selsey Bill from Bosham and drop anchor at the sailing club.

The nurse went to the ladies'. While she was gone Pelham's brigadier leant over his double Scotch and leered in a fatherly way.

'A charmer,' he said. 'Half your luck, you young bucks.'

'Well, sir . . .'

'Come now. You don't mean to say you don't find her . . .?'

'I remind her too much of her brother. That's it, sir. I've been trying to tell her, well in that case . . . if you can't think of me as anything but a brother . . .'

'I understand perfectly. Life's too short, Pelham. For me more than you.'

They drank.

The brigadier said, 'In that case, if you really want to extricate yourself . . .'

'Oh, I do, sir.'

'I could drop the lady back to her billet. She can't come to trouble with an old man like me.'

'I'd be very grateful, sir.'

Pelham lowered his voice. 'I believe she'd be quite pleased too.'

The brigadier coughed. 'I say, I think you're just being nice.'

Pelham moulded his dark face, his more or less delicate features, into lines of ferocious honesty. It was a stunt that had always worked well with senior consultants at St Bartholomew's.

'I think it's immoral to be nice in these matters.'

'Quite.' The brigadier drank. His lips sputtered with delight on the rim of the glass. He said, 'That thing you applied for . . .'

'Yes, sir?'

'You said you wanted lots of cutting experience. This could give you heaps of cutting.'

'I see.'

'You can use a parachute?'

'I trained with a parachute division.'

'Don't think for a second I'm favouring you. Only three other young chaps applied.'

'The job? What is it, sir?'

'It's across the Adriatic. You'll be treating Yugoslavs. Loads of cutting, really.'

'I thought the country had all gone to the enemy.'

'More or less. It's a complicated question.' The girl from Littlehampton was back and the brigadier smiled sideways at her. 'The chap I spoke to is an expert. He says you'll certainly survive. He'll be in contact . . .'

After excusing himself, Pelham went to another bar, found other friends, but did not drink much, being now in training. Nonetheless, he felt light at heart: his young life had been rescued from futility.

The next morning he gave anaesthetics. An operation on a tank driver with depressed skull fracture. A few appendectomies. Towards the end of the list someone knocked on the operating theatre door and a nurse went to see who it was. Returning, she faced Pelham, mask to mask, at the oxygen machine.

There was an officer to see him urgently in the Registrar's office. The surgeon said he should go. An orderly called Fielding would look after the rest of the business.

Pelham dumped his cap, gown, mask and gloves in the sterilizing room and crossed the quadrangle under a bright autumn sun. As soon as he entered the office, the Registrar rose and exited leaving a rakish officer behind. A man with a limp and almost certainly, a wooden leg. He wore a shirt of Hawaiian design under a loose leather jerkin to which his major's crowns were sewn.

'You're an acting captain now,' he said. 'Okay?'

'Yes, sir.'

'My name's Rankin. I administer Force 147. We can do what we like, we happen to be under the Foreign Office. No one but General Alexander has the right to tell us anything at all. How does that strike you?'

'I'm very envious.'

'No need to be. Part of it now. You. You can *jump* though?'

'Yes.'

'Good. You're being sent to the Yugoslavs. But not to Yugoslavs as such. Nothing so simple.'

Rankin's eye blinked madly, perhaps a symptom of the enthusiasm for the Balkan question. The laziness of his voice did not completely convince one of his disinterest. 'Do you know anything about Yugoslavia?'

'Nothing.'

'Well, it's something like this. When the enemy invaded the country, the Yugoslavs fragmented . . . broke up, as it were . . . into three groups. One group were the Croatian lunatics called Ustachi, led by a poisonous little man called Pavelich. They co-operated with the Germans from the start and continue to do so. Pavelich has his reward. He is President of an Ustachi Croatia. The Ustachi are bedfellows, politically speaking, of the Nazis, and they detest most other Yugoslavs, especially Serbs and Muslims. Just as an example, they massacred 300,000 Serbs in Zagreb in 1941 – an awful lot of people in anyone's language.'

From politeness, Pelham agreed it was a staggering number. To him it was still like a statistic from a news broadcast.

'So, first the Ustachi. Next, those elements of the Royal Yugoslav Army who resisted the enemy. They are led by a staff officer called Mikhailevich. A wonderful man, I've spent a lot of time with him.' (At this point Rankin, as if unconsciously, felt his artificial leg.) 'Mikhailevich's people are called Chetniks. The trouble is that poor old Draža – I mean, Mikhailevich – began to co-operate passively with the enemy. Whenever

German soldiers were ambushed, the Germans exacted a ferocious toll in hostages. For example, at a city called Kragujevac the Germans shot all males over fifteen years old. Seven thousand men, the total came to. So Draža approached the Germans and said, let's exist together, there are too many ordinary people getting shot. There's no doubt Draža means to stab the bastards in the back eventually. But eventually isn't quite good enough. So goodbye to the Chetniks. With regret.'

And certainly Rankin seemed to mourn them for a second or two, as if they were more his style of people.

'The third group,' he went on, 'are actively fighting and destroying the enemy and damn the cost. Unlike the Chetniks, they have only just begun to receive help from us. You, dear chap, are part of the help. This group arm and clothe themselves with what they take from the corpses of the enemy. Their leader is a former private – God help us! – in the Austro-Hungarian Army. His nickname is Tito, his headquarters are in Bosnia for the moment. His army call themselves the Partisanka, the partisans. This Tito has not only made a guerrilla army but organized a rough civil and political set-up as well. You'll meet him soon. Him and dear Moja Javich.'

'Moja . . .?'

'She'll be your mentor. She has a way of being everyone's mentor. Charming lady. Cosmopolite. Speaks English, German, French, Russian . . . one of that type. Now come and meet the girls.'

'The girls?'

'Yes. You know, those endearing things that surrounded you in your boyhood.'

Outside a car waited, driver at wheel. A red plaque on its bumper bar, and on the plaque a gilt crown and three gilt pips.

Rankin said, 'A certain brigadier insisted you must have the use of that. God knows how you came to merit it.'

It seems, thought Pelham, the girl from Littlehampton was

to the brigadier's taste.

They drove south. The light was strong, the sea a proper Adriatic blue. Bland as the annual report of a fraudulent stock company. For over there, the Croats and Serbians worked their atrocities, and so did the astounding Germans. Since he would soon be amidst all this, he now thought: where does all the blood wash to?

As if strange Major Rankin was thinking on similar lines, he jerked a thumb towards the Murgian mountains above the coastal plain.

'Cannae over there. You know, where Hannibal killed 70,000 men in an afternoon. Even today's experts could hardly manage that, eh?'

He shifted his non-leg on the carpeted floor of the brigadier's vehicle.

'By the way, David. You should know that if a British soldier or anyone else is found in . . . what shall we say? . . . *commerce* with a partisan woman, he is simply shot. They're quick on the draw when it comes to chastity.'

'I'll be careful.'

'Do be. Very. And always use precautions, eh? That's the chap. Because if a partisan woman is found pregnant . . . well! My friends call me *Twinkum* by the way.'

Pelham let the nickname sink slowly in his mind. It had to it the very smell of the wanton Mayfair of the thirties, the mad rituals of the 'season', the prescriptive strawberries at Wimbledon, the necessary *Brut* at Ascot. None of which had done anything to prevent the whole world growing tumours, region by region. *Twinkum*, the very word, spoke of an interstice of life to which Pelham's family half belonged. Pelham himself had been both enchanted and sickened by it. The Welsh blood from his mother's side and his medical studies had both helped to prevent him from becoming a full-fledged Twinkum.

'What are their reasons?' he asked after a while.

'For their ban on romance? I don't quite know. Remember our Roundheads? All revolutionaries are a bit strait-laced, and communists . . .'

'Are these Partisanka communist?'

'In a manner. Tito is. Look, David, their politics aren't our concern, it's what they're doing to the old Reich, eh? Now Moja, she's no communist.'

'I don't care about their politics. I simply asked for my own information, Twinkum.'

But inevitably, the Marxism of his new comrades across the Adriatic made him feel a little more at risk.

The villa of Force 147 at Mola stood on a slight headland above the sea. It had a high white wall and there were many palm trees and fountains in the garden – some of them so much as spraying water. Pelham noticed a commando in full kit, with automatic weapon, half hidden behind a bird bath.

Inside there was no sign of orderlies, clerks, sergeant-majors or any of the other functionaries one expects to find behind the front door of a Force headquarters. In a panelled hallway, Twinkum Rankin pushed an unmarked door open. In armchairs and by mantelpieces were half a dozen individual-looking officers in the Twinkum mould. He was not surprised at them.

It was the girls who surprised him. They were all seven of them long-boned superb beings. Summer dresses. Sheer stockings. Congenital drawls. Lustrous hair. Pelham wondered what entrepreneur had got them here, so cool and well-laundered, only a few weeks after the enemy had left.

A lean girl with dark hair and dark eyes approached Major Rankin.

'Twinkum,' she said, 'they rang from the Foreign Office.'

'Oh?'

'Something about the Yate-say personage. I made a note somewhere. Now don't forget to look for it.'

She looked at Pelham wryly. Though she could have been only twenty-two or three, there was in her, as in many elegant girls, a sort of seniority that could intimidate a person.

Her name was Caroline Sestwick. Who was he? Rankin said, 'He's the Yate-say personage.'

'Good heavens. I thought he'd be at least thirty-five.'

Pelham said, 'I'm old enough to be your elder brother.'

'*Brother!* What an idea!'

Laughing, Twinkum embraced her very closely. Pelham felt a stab of loss in his stomach and some sexual hostility.

'You must stop being a Nefertiti and a minx, my precious,' Twinkum told the girl.

'I'll get you a drink,' the girl promised Pelham from within the caresses of Twinkum. 'What?'

'Scotch and water. And please call me David.'

And God, he thought, you're no Littlehampton Ophelia. Whose Daddy dies behind the arras because the Saturday flannels-brigade snub him.

The other girls and officers had gone on chatting clannishly and sipping at their gin. Their indifference to his entry was a badge of class. So too the off-hand eccentricity of the officers and the sharp low laughter of the soft-fibred girls.

'This,' Twinkum honked out for all their benefits, 'is David Pelham. The first-aid man to Josip.'

Someone said, 'Good God.'

'Julia,' said Twinkum. 'Sarah. Elspeth. Caroline you know. Margaret. Antonia. Hester.'

And so Twinkum's lovely solar system were given their names.

'Then there's Jimmy, Jumbo, Tibby, Jason, Ginger and Tim.'

He could have been naming a litter of kittens.

The girl called Caroline returned with his drink.

'You said something about Yate-say,' Pelham asked Twinkum. The girl remained at their side.

'We call it Yate-say. It's spelt Jajce. It's a town in Bosnia. You may see it soon.'

'May I?'

Caroline said, 'It's Tito's headquarters.'

'I see. It just seems . . .'

'What?' said Twinkum.

'Well, perhaps a little risky to use the . . .'

'Use the real name of the place?' Twinkum suggested.

'Yes.'

'My boy,' Twinkum said. 'That's exactly why we let only a very reliable class of people in here.'

A little reddish man, wearing the same sort of peasant jerkin as Major Rankin, came in to Pelham's side. 'I can sell you a battalion supply of razor blades if you'd care for them. A nugatory price. You can buy almost anything in Yugoslavia with razor blades. Excellent currency. Light to carry.'

Twinkum contradicted this. 'Cigarettes,' he said. 'We'll get him a company's supply of cigarettes. He can't carry more than that.'

Ginger persisted. 'There isn't a country in the world where razor blades are scarcer than in Yugoslavia. Also, half the women have beards.'

They all laughed.

'Every ounce I carry would surely be medical supplies.'

Twinkum winced. 'That's the problem, David. We can manage ordinary supplies but we haven't as yet infiltrated medical stores.'

'Never mind. I can get a letter from brigade. Then I'll just trot round ordering stores. If you tell me how much I can take in pounds weight . . .'

'But they won't give you anything, David. You see, you can't tell the people in stores where you're going. All medical supplies have to be written off to a particular unit, because the big chaps are terribly worried about a drug black market.'

Thinking of *his* brigadier, Pelham perhaps made a complacent face. So that Twinkum suddenly became severe.

'Believe me, David, we've looked into this. All you'll have are any personal supplies of sulpha, morphine and so on, you can scrounge from the hospital. The partisans have supplies of ether, lint, plaster. They take it from the enemy. Like everything they have. You see, as I said, we haven't begun properly supplying them . . .'

It seemed to Pelham that the major's hands were quivering and there was certainly sweat on his face. At the same time Pelham was aware that the others were also watching Twinkum.

'Plaster of Paris,' Twinkum said. 'They're very keen on plaster of Paris. It's their cure-all.'

'Or their kill-all,' Ginger said softly. As if to ease Twinkum's sudden sweating.

Somewhere in the villa a gong was rung.

'Lunch,' a girl sang.

At the lunch table they ate lobster caught overnight in the Adriatic. No one spoke to Twinkum for a while, instead letting him recover at the head of the table. He ate quickly and drank his wine absently. At the end of the second course he stood up.

'Girls and boys,' he said. 'Excuse me, the call of the in-tray, you know.'

Caroline and Pelham sat either side of him. He added something only they could hear. 'I don't need you this afternoon, my precious. Be a darling and show David about.'

And then for Pelham's sake alone: 'David, I know you won't misunderstand . . . this isn't a seraglio. The girls are aesthetic as well as terribly helpful. They are also from very good families . . .'

Twinkum fondled Pelham's shoulder a little. This small intimacy was, for some reason, repellent. Perhaps because I

23

want his girl, Pelham thought.

'I won't take liberties, Twinkum.'

'Well, my dear fellow, not so much that. More a matter of the spirit in which things are broached. Wouldn't you say?'

They walked in the garden and on the beach, and, at mid-afternoon, drank tea on a terrace beneath the silent villa. The sun was bright. If the tea had not been served by a commando they would not have been reminded of the iron deadly winter coming soon to the battlefields of the north and the fabulous hills of Bosnia.

'A remarkable man,' David ventured. 'Twinkum.'

'Oh yes.'

He studied the texture of her skin.

'Was he ill at lunch?' He felt uneasy, as if he were taking advantage of a sick man in asking the question. Caroline's face went on looking translucent to a depth of half an inch. 'He seemed a little feverish,' he persisted.

'He'd be all right still. If he were over there. It's when you bring that sort of man back and sit them down with all the comforts that they start shivering.'

'He was with that other Yugoslav chap?'

'Yes. Draža. Mikhailevich. Twinkum's a disappointed man, you see. Because the Draža thing went sour. Draža softened up. It's a tragedy really. Twinkum hates communism but has to do business with this Tito.'

'Did he lose his leg over there?'

'The first half of it, to below the knee. He was with the Chetniks. All the Yugoslavs who were with Twinkum have left Draža now and joined Tito. To Twinkum it's a bit like losing your family.'

'The operation was done by a Yugoslav?'

'Twinkum's? To below the knee, yes. Then they covered it up with plaster of Paris – no padding underneath. It suppurated,

24

of course. There it was, trying to swell inside plaster of Paris. Can you imagine? They cut the plaster away – without an anaesthetic, he told me once. By then he was good for nothing. They carried him down to the coast and got him off by submarine to Egypt. Once army doctors looked at him, they took off the rest of the leg to the hip.'

'You seem to know him well,' Pelham said, offering her the plate of cake.

'Well, he's my cousin.'

'Oh.' He watched her hands, the just perceptible pink of the veins. 'I see. I thought that you were perhaps fiancés.'

'Good God, no. Twinkum is one of those nice queers.' She laughed as languid and erotic a laugh as he could have wished for, but it mocked him too. 'I mean, you could have guessed, couldn't you? It would take a nice queer to dream up a barracks like this, a friendly brotherly place and not a house of ill-fame. Now you, David, you would never have done it.'

'Perhaps I lack the imagination . . .'

'Also,' she said, 'you'd be always mauling the personnel.'

'I want to maul the personnel now,' he said, using that look of hopeless honesty he'd tried out on the brigadier.

Her hand reached out and slapped his. 'Well, you must control yourself. You can't give way at the tea table.'

Her hand returned and she frowned. 'You might as well know what Twinkum said. It was yesterday. He said, that boy's going to have to deal with dreadful wounds, wounds you wouldn't believe.'

'Listen here, Caroline, don't I interest you a little?'

'For the moment we have orders to look about. Let's look about. It's no good acting on impulse.'

All afternoon they walked about, he lightly touching her white elbow. He was forced to admit, unhurried possession and the promise of the night are much better than a hectic fumble amongst the teacakes.

In the morning it was raining, but Pelham felt full of business. All the girls were up breakfasting or at work. Caroline had left him at dawn to shower, dress and (so she said) catch up on letters.

David planned to see his brigadier. He couldn't believe he would be given no supplies at all. He sent a message for the brigadier's car and driver to fetch him at the door at half past nine. While he waited, looking at the wet garden, the officer called Ginger found him.

'Pushing off for the Imperiale?'

'No. I'm going to see a brigadier I know. About medical stores.'

'Forlorn, my boy. But I'll come with you if you like.'

In the car, Pelham studied a phrase book of Serbo-Croat Twinkum had given him the night before. Ginger, smoking, told him, 'It's all very easy. *Engleski*, English. *Šlivovica*, slivovitz. *Ushi*, lice. What's hospital? *Bolnica*! *Bolnica*, hospital. *Avioni*, aircraft. *Pokret*, enemy. *Hemendeks*, ham and eggs . . .'

'You're not serious.'

'Yes, *hemendeks*. But of course it's not all so simple. *Da*, yes. *Nov*, no. And pain is *boli*.'

The brigadier was not happy to see them. It seemed he considered the unspoken debt had been paid with car and driver. He said, 'You have to understand, all we've been authorized to do is send a doctor. We've provided a doctor and fed him into the 147 system.'

'But hold on,' Ginger kept telling him. 'Hold on. It isn't like a cottage hospital over there. A planeload of lint alone wouldn't be enough.'

'We've all seen badly wounded men, Captain.'

'Have we just?'

'I don't think this is fruitful,' said Pelham, but it was useless speaking. The brigadier and Ginger were locked into their mutual aggression.

'I don't know what you mean,' said the brigadier. 'Also, I must remind you, Captain, there are ways of talking to a senior officer.'

'Lawrence of Arabia was a captain, but he knew his Arabs better than any general. At 147 we know our bloody Arabs and that's what we're for, and we owe nobody but the Foreign Office any kow-tows. I can therefore get away with calling you Pox-head, Maggoty-balls, Arse-features. Be grateful I don't.'

The brigadier made a face of distaste and turned to Pelham. 'We know it will require improvisation, David, that's why we chose your sort of man.'

'Then can I have an orderly, sir?'

'I'll insist on your having an appropriate orderly.'

'Sergeant Fielding, sir. A bachelor, steady, has parachute training. Might be hard to extricate from base hospital.'

'We'll get him, David. I'll see to that. Here's an authorization from me to Quartermaster, Base Medical Stores. But I fear it's worthless. Perhaps you could unleash your aggressive friend on them.'

'I'll wait outside for you, David,' said Ginger, and belched off-handedly, and went.

The brigadier shook David's hand and muttered valedictory things. It occurred to Pelham: he half expects me to be killed. But this morning he couldn't believe that there would not be, forever, Caroline Sestwicks to be sought, and a David Pelham to do the seeking.

Till mid-afternoon they argued at the stores. By three o'clock they'd acquired a badly-hinged portable operating table. Pelham did not consider it worth taking on the journey. He had also been given a surgical pannier containing ether, pentothal, morphia, gauze, packages of ligatures and some instruments. By three o'clock his mind was on tea and Caroline. He thought, am I really tough enough for this journey? The atmosphere of 147, implying that Yugoslav wounds are essentially the bloodiest, that there were unguessed-at dimensions of barbarity over there, had got into his system and undermined him a little.

Ginger borrowed a motor-bike from someone and raced back to his desk at Mola. Before going, he said, 'Moja Javich will provide. She's the great improviser. Twinkum swears by her. She's in the wrong army of course, as far as Twinkum's concerned. A partisan. She found him raving in a country clinic – his leg chopped off. He'd been shot by a Chetnik – he never mentions that. A bit of an embarrassment to them, Twinkum was, once they started getting on with the Germans. So it was Moja who found him and got him out. He said she could slip into some tiny village and find anything she wanted, a truck or medicine. I think Twinkum was quite taken with Mrs Javich.' But the name had no comfort for Pelham. He thought, I'm losing Caroline for some large crafty peasant.

Alone he went to the hospital. There he persuaded a number of medical officers to prescribe double doses of medication for their patients. These went, not into the patients, but into the boot of the brigadier's car. Benzedrine, sulpha, more morphine, iodine tablets and so on. But no penicillin. There were special rules about dispensing that. Therefore, no wonder drugs for the partisans.

In the corridor of the hospital he found Sergeant Fielding and asked him what he thought of a posting to Yugoslavia. Fielding listened with the growing radiance of a shy man who considers life has not moved fast enough, but now has hopes that it will pick up pace.

That night, when they were all drinking coffee in the mess at the villa, Pelham again intent on Caroline's skin textures, there was a call for him.

'Pelham?'

'Yes.'

'Colonel Ash, Base Hospital. I have received a movement order signed by the divisional commander for an F. N. Fielding, Sergeant, RAMC'

'Yes, sir.'

'You're taking him off to the Balkans.'

'He is going with me, sir.'

'I suppose you think this is a great joke.'

'No, sir. I need a strong orderly.'

'Don't think I have any time for you after this, Pelham.'

'Very well.'

'I am consultant orthopaedic surgeon at Barts and an examiner at the College of Surgeons.'

'Yes I know, sir.'

'If we both survive the war, I would advise you not to come near Barts or the board of examiners at the College of Surgeons.'

Professional vendettas sickened Pelham. Some of the frustration of the day stirred in him. 'Sir, if we both survive I'll go where I bloody want.'

'I'll have this movement countermanded.'

'Sir, I suggest you speak to the OC Force 147.' He stood back from the receiver. Why pester poor Twinkum, he thought.

'Ginger!' he called. 'There's a Pox-head here to be spoken to.'

Chapter 2 The General in Bosnia

Three nights later Pelham jumped from a Halifax bomber into the howling air above a Bosnian field ringed by bonfires. Jumping with him was not only Fielding but an Irish commando called Private Cleary, a much-demoted savage who had been assigned to David as batman-cum-bodyguard.

Landing, Pelham was embraced by smelly men and – could it be? . . . yes, women. They were all badly dressed in what proved to be fragments of German, Italian and Ustachi uniforms. Their affection was violent – he was no small man, yet they span him from person to person. Their excesses bore out everything Twinkum had said of them. They had him choking down a mug of rakia before Cleary had as much as touched the ground.

Later, Pelham would understand their ferocious affection for him. He had never seen a battle wound in its first gushing seconds. He had never seen a battle wound which had been let rot for months. He had never seen the outrages of Yugoslav medicine. Therefore he did not understand why they spent time hugging him in an exposed and perhaps dangerous field.

A middle-aged man, more restrained than the others, took Pelham's hand, saying simply, 'Major Kallich. Welcome to our country.' The surgical pannier landed close by. They loaded it on a donkey. Pelham could see Private Cleary drinking great mouthfuls of liquor and saying, for some reason,

'It's good to meet Christians again.' No doubt the welcome must have been pleasant to a man who'd been twice demoted and once jailed.

Quiet Fielding had doubled his ankle on landing, but refused to ride on one of the pack animals. They marched that night in the wooded hills. Even in such darkness, Pelham was aware of the concentration of all the marchers around him, their senses vigilant all night. At dawn they got to a deserted farm on high ground.

A partisan officer, very young, perhaps eighteen, pointed them up the ladder out of the stony farmyard. They climbed into the loft and spread their blankets.

'Look,' Cleary said, gaping out the loft door, 'from up here you can see the road along the valley. And a bridge. They're not as silly as they look.'

Fielding, whose ankle was paining him and who had been a schoolteacher, said pedantically, 'I don't understand what you mean.'

'Well, they can see any mechanized movement from up here.'

'That seems pretty ordinary military sense to me,' said Fielding, wincing at his ankle.

'It is, it is. But don't you always get a shock when furriners work these things out for themselves?'

Pelham said to Fielding, 'I'm going to bandage your ankle.'

'No, sir. A bad policy. To treat ourselves first.'

'If you ride a donkey the rest of the way I'll have to do a haemorrhoidectomy on you. Cleary, get the pannier brought up.'

In this way Pelham began his mission to the partisans by treating his own orderly. He used an elastic bandage, since – unlike other materials – it could be used again.

He had been up all night and most of the night before. He thought, it isn't the battle surgery itself that frightens me. It's

31

my untidiness. I find it hard enough to pack a kit bag tidily. Untidiness is worse than inexperience. Fielding has a gift for organization. He is a proper old woman, thank God.

Pelham said, 'Best to keep your boot on while you sleep. If we can get it on.'

You got to the loft by a sturdy rustic ladder outside. There were noises on this ladder as he battled with Fielding's ammunition boot. The middle-aged man who had welcomed him to Yugoslavia was at the door, knocking. 'Gentlemen,' he said, 'could I interest you in breakfast?' He carried two bottles of spirits. He was bald and broad-faced. Behind him came two orderlies, one with loaves of black bread and plates, the other with a tureen of thick soup.

'Major Ante Kallich,' the middle-aged man said. 'I was in the grocery business in Cleveland for nineteen years. They call me Tony. I meet all distinguished guests because these other fellers . . . you ought to hear their English! Even the General himself isn't so hot.'

The major wore a German officer's tunic. On its sleeve an embroidered sprig of edelweiss.

They sat round a chest and ate Pelham's first Balkan breakfast – harsh soup, heavy black bread and a little more than half a dozen measures of slivovitz.

'So much,' said Fielding, 'for the Anglo-Saxon idea. That there's an hour of the day before which it isn't decent to take liquor.'

Pelham slept soundly on that cold hilltop all day. Or if he woke it was for seconds only. He would listen to the wind in the pine forests and the lazy conversations of the Yugoslav sentries. Their voices sounded secure in their control of the countryside and helped drug him to sleep again.

When he woke finally he saw Fielding sitting against the wall, watching him. Pelham said, 'You'll have to take aspirin before we start off again.'

Fielding said, 'There was a convoy on the road. An artillery battery. Twenty guns.'

'When?'

'An hour ago. It brings it home to you. That you're in occupied territory. You know.'

Private Cleary did not appear until it was time for the evening meal. He climbed into the loft after Kallich and went to Pelham's side. His machine-carbine shone as if it had been enthusiastically cleaned and oiled only a second before.

He said, 'These fellers are the real rebels! The IRA aren't the fluff in a rebel's ear compared to these fellers.'

Kallich said, 'We'll be there before dawn.'

They ate, chatted, drank till nine o'clock. By then the rakia had worked on them, taking the distress out of the idea of walking all night.

The major told them interesting things. He had returned to his boyhood village in 1932 and, with the earnings from his American business, became a local grandee. At the beginning of the war he'd been a captain in some local militia unit. In 1941 when the country was occupied, the German command gave Montenegro into the keeping of the Italians. The Montenegrins had always bucked in the face of invasion and knew how to use the hills. The Italians panicked. 'They were pretty hard on my boy,' Kallich said. Kallich's boy had had literary ambitions, wrote some nationalist poetry and published it anonymously in an underground paper. He was full of the joy of authorship. The Italians arrested the editor and tortured him for the names of all his contributors.

They called at the Kallich house while the major was away.

'My son they hanged in the living room. My wife, naturally, tried to fight them off with a hunting rifle and was bayoneted to death.'

No one spoke. Except, eventually, Kallich. 'There's something you've got to understand – everyone in the partisans has a story like that. That's no big-time story. Except to me.'

The others continued speechless. Again, it was Kallich's duty to continue the conversation. 'Anyhow, the Italians made peace earlier this month. So be it. I was very surprised at them in Montenegro. In the US, they were always kind of pleasant.'

The travelling that night was very cold. Pelham stumbled along in a daze and the wind blew sharply. After midnight Kallich halted the column outside a town in which a few lights still burned. A local man came out of the darkness and spoke to the major, who in turn spoke to Pelham.

'There's a German signal unit staying in a priest's house at the west end of the town. This man is going to take us on a detour.'

'Who is he?' Pelham asked. The whole warning had a Judas smell to him – perhaps because his stomach was unsettled, and the liquor had burned itself out in his body.

'He's the mayor.'

'If there are Germans there, they might be holding his family hostage.'

'Yeah, doctor? Let me tell you: he's in the same position as me when it comes to family.'

Pelham felt foolish and followed the bereaved mayor. Rain began to fall. There was no ambush.

Towards four o'clock the clouds shifted and they marched by moonlight. Then, in the dawn, they came to a strong river with rough-hewn water mills thick along its shores. The hills around were steep, and from a sloping pass between them they saw a terraced town, a weir, a castle.

'Big Josip lives up there,' Kallich told Pelham.

The major said Cleary and Fielding would be taken to breakfast at the hospital. But Pelham was to breakfast with the general.

'Hospital?' Pelham said. 'I didn't think you had one.'

'We didn't. Till just lately.'

'I was sent here to make a hospital.'

'Yeah. There's been a bit of a mix-up.'

'What do you mean?'

'Look, it's going to be made right.'

'So there's already a hospital. With beds and an operating theatre?'

'And a Vienna-trained doctor. Not like your average town-and-country Yugoslav quack. Come and see General Tito.'

'Yes. I should say I'd bloody well want to!'

He could see himself giving anaesthetics and being surgeon's-mate again. I could have stayed in Bari, with all the comforts of Caroline.

The wet streets rose steeply to Tito's castle. They met a few early-morning dogs cocking legs against the grey houses and very old women and white-faced children moving quietly uphill.

'Where are they going?' Pelham asked.

'To mass.'

'I thought you were all communists.'

'We can't be too extreme. There's a Franciscan priest on Tito's staff. You're pretty upset, aren't you? You don't want to work with Dr Grubich?'

'It isn't what I came for.'

Audibly the major lost patience.

'Listen, pal. You're on our payroll now. And don't think you're the only superior Limey who's come prancing up this hill.'

'Go to hell.'

There were sentries at the bridge into Jajce castle. They waved casually at Kallich. The archway they entered became a tunnel. Pelham felt certain it was carrying them downwards, perhaps to a command post under the ground. Instead they came out in a sunken garden. The weeds stood shoulder high amongst damp cypresses. Another sentry kept watch at the bottom of steps leading to a balcony.

This is the most comfortless place there is, Pelham thought. It was the sort of place that convinced you the Middle Ages must have been dismal, even for the Lords of Bosnia.

Kallich knocked at a door on the balcony, yelled his name and entered. There were three men at table. Two bottles of spirits had been set down for their breakfast, as well as a pot of thick gruel and the everlasting black bread. A middle-aged man stood up and silently took Pelham by the shoulder and hand. He had a firm Slavic face.

Kallich said, 'This is General Tito.'

The two other men also rose. One (Pelham discovered in the end) was Tito's chief of staff, the other chairman of the Jajce Ogbor or Council. The chairman of the council presented Pelham with a glass of spirits. Tito, the chief of staff, and Kallich all smiled. Tito muttered, 'My confrère!' and sought his own glass and held it up towards Pelham. Everyone made grunts of applause. Some of the rakia was drunk, in unison.

'Wel-come!' said Tito, like a command. He pointed at chairs Pelham and Kallich were to pullup to the table. Then David sat down with the others and had a plate of soup put before him. There were no waiters and the general wore a grey coat with no insignia. Pelham could imagine that the gallant Twinkum might feel uncomfortable here.

Tito spoke in Serbo-Croat and Kallich translated.

Tito: You are a partisan now.

And they drank.

Pelham: I'm very happy to be here except that I was told that I was needed, that I was to organize a hospital. Yet I learn from comrade Kallich that there's a well-established hospital here, run by a doctor senior to me in qualifications. It is very distressing.

The general replied, a pleasant and sonorous voice. Kallich

transmitted the meaning, sentence by sentence.

'I have been asking your government for help since early this year. After we were visited by a liaison mission led by Major Fitzroy Maclean, they have at last begun to send some supplies. You come in answer to my request for a doctor. Since the allies agreed to send a doctor, Professor Grubich has come to us. If I had radioed the allies and said, no I don't need a doctor in Jajce, I'll discover some other place he can go, there would have been delay and all the sense of urgency would have died out. So I let the arrangements proceed . . .'

Pelham said, 'It seems that the general might have a further place in mind for me to go?'

The general, spooning soup and drinking spirits, spoke again. There was a peasant quality in the way he handled food and conversation together.

'Somewhere more important even than this.'

'Might I ask where that is?'

'An island off the coast. Before the end of the year, before the end of the month maybe, we're going to lose our ports on the coast, we're going to be encircled here. It always happens. For a time we occupied north Serbia, for a time west Serbia, for a time Montenegro, but we will always find it hard to hold territory permanently until the allies open other fronts, or the Russians invade from Hungary and Rumania. Since both of these things will happen in the end, we don't worry too much, we keep our running shoes handy . . .'

For principle's sake, Pelham still frowned. He was in fact thinking of the villa in Mola, of Twinkum and Ginger instructing him in how Tito was brilliant, adaptable, convinced of his immortality, and physically brave amongst a race of lunatically brave men. You could tell that what they had said was true, even from the way he broke his black bread. When Twinkum began trembling you knew his bravery in Yugoslavia had been the result of forcing himself close to his limits. Watching Tito however you knew he had bravery to burn, enough to last a war of thirty years.

Tito continued talking. 'A few islands off the coast – these we can hold permanently . . . perhaps. They can be our back door, our only door. They can be a refuge for our wounded. You can have your hospital there. You can be chairman of the board.' Pelham always remembered the slight mockery that sat in Tito's smile as Kallich translated this sentiment.

Pelham said, 'Could the general tell me how long before I go?'

'A week or two at the most. You should have no trouble travelling at night. Major Maclean made the same journey only a few weeks back. You must speak to Dr Grubich and learn as much as you can about dealing with wounded people in large quantities. As an assistant you will have as good a person as I can give you. She is Moja Javich.' The chief of staff and the chairman laughed warmly when the name was spoken. It was not mocking, it was not sexual. Not, in any case, the sort of sexual laughter that rises amongst men when obviously erotic women are named.

'One warning,' Tito and Kallich said. 'Don't expect it to be a big island. Don't expect a Brač. Don't expect a Hvar.'

Everyone laughed companionably. Tito said, 'Eat with us then.'

Obeying, Pelham felt euphoria enter his body with the rakia. It hasn't been futile and I am eating with Homeric men.

The hospital had clearly been an institution used to beds, not a convert from education like the hospital in Bari. It was penitential, a little like an asylum or a workhouse. Its walls were plain and heavy, its ceilings high.

The professor was drinking coffee in his office. He had just finished his morning rounds. He had a strong face and was about fifty years old. 'Come,' he said, 'a hospital tour. The place is all tidy.' His English was American. He led Pelham by the hand out into the corridor. He knocked at an office door.

A fair-haired woman opened it. If you had seen her face on the streets of London you would have presumed she was Scandinavian. Beneath her brown overall the body was small and trim and you expected a green-eyed, tilt-nosed pert face to go with it. In fact the face was broad, the nose classic, the lips long. The blue eyes glistened with a maternal irony, even for Grubich. Pelham saw this and was influenced to look on her as a matron instead of as a young woman. It was the eyes that said forty even if all else said younger.

'Moja. The Englishman doctor. Please explain to him the works while round we go. Whaddyasay?'

The woman sought Pelham's hand. 'I am Moja Javich. We're going to work together,' she said.

'They talk about you in Italy,' said Pelham. But their talk had not prepared him for a woman so neatly made.

'Twinkum and the others,' she snorted. 'What they tell you is pure legend.'

'You speak English so well,' Pelham told her.

She looked mocking as Tito had earlier. 'Look, mother, they talk just like humans.'

'I didn't mean it that way,' Pelham warned her. He could tell she would try teasing the life out of his Anglo-Saxon niceties.

'Let us show you the hospital.' So, at home with Moja and in the company of the professor, he moved into the wards and detected more strongly than in any polite or military hospital he had ever entered the wolfish smell of death.

'Tell him, please,' Professor Grubich instructed Moja, stopping by a bed. Moja explained the case to Pelham. 'This boy was bayoneted through the jaws. Both sides do that a lot as a refinement. He was on the run for three weeks. There were complications . . .'

'Osteomyelitis,' Grubich supplied.

'Yes,' said Moja. 'The maggots that infested the wound prevented septicaemia. Quite a number of wounded who come to us have had their lives saved by maggot infestation. However, the maggots went on to invade the left sinus. It has been drained, the boy is on sulpha drugs. The professor suspects some brain damage.'

'How old is he?' Pelham asked.

'Fourteen years.'

The boy slept. Pelham looked at the swollen cheeks above the dressings. He was naïve enough to think, well, star patient first. Soon we'll see the commissars in to have their plantar warts removed. Certainly there were some simple pneumonia cases, a child with an appendectomy, a half dozen broken ankles. There were as many amputations, and a few shell fragment wounds of minor importance. But many beds of chest and stomach wounds. A girl with the pinched anxious look of the dying. Her colleagues stretched near her, at least a dozen, all pinched about the mouth and nose. That look was called *hippocratic facies*. It was the useless revolt of living cells against the crucial organs, which had already voted for death.

At a given bed a thin young woman was taking pulses and watching a bottle of blood empty into her patient.

'The doctor wants me to explain this case,' Moja said. 'He's proud of it. A machine-gun wound straight through the rib cage. A clean wound. It punctured the inferior lobe of the left lung but the repairs were successful. The professor is using silver drainage tubes to drain the area and prevent lung oedema. This one, he says, is going to live.'

Pelham said, 'These people were all wounded recently.' It was a medical conclusion he had come to.

'Of course. They were brought here yesterday afternoon. They met an enemy advance guard in a village forty kilometres from Jajce. The enemy was well equipped.'

40

'With wounds like these? You say they were carried forty kilometres?'

'In hammocks made of blankets. They've no Grubichs there, you see.'

Grubich went on smiling slightly, thrusting a questioning, paternal face in the direction of the man who might live. Meanwhile Moja put a long and well-kept hand on the sleeve of Pelham's battle dress. 'My dear, don't think of it in English terms. You'll lose your mind that way.'

David shrugged off this little intimacy, half-maternal, half-flirtatious as it was. 'Where do you get the drugs?'

Moving from him, she translated *that* for Grubich and they laughed together at the foreigner.

'Our only continuing supply is spoils from attacks on garrisons. Plundered sick bays, doctor We also receive an excellent stream of supplies from harlots who are sympathizers.'

'You mean, they make German soldiers pay in . . . in medical supplies?'

'Exactly.'

'Isn't that a dangerous demand to make of a German soldier?'

'Of course. Girls have to pick their mark. It's always a dangerous thing. Having commerce with foreign soldiers.'

She raised her eyebrows at him in a very stylized manner. It was as if she would not tolerate that anyone should forget she was elegant and feminine.

At the end of the ward stood a bed apart from the others. Here Moja and Grubich became thoughtful. Grubich felt the pulse of the boy who lay there, his face covered with dressings arranged around an antique metal trumpet that rose straight from his wounded face It was some sort of catheter to help him breathe. It didn't seem to be a sterile arrangement.

'He's a German officer,' Moja said. 'He won't live. He has thoracic wounds and his face is best not mentioned.'

41

Pelham wanted to say, he's only a child. His ears looked adolescent, even if violet.

Moja went on. 'They brought him to Jajce with nine others to be questioned. When the questioning was over they marched them round the far side of the hill and made them dig a grave and then executed them. That's the way things are done in Yugoslavia.'

Pelham felt a rush of bile in his throat.

'This boy . . . ?'

'This boy was executed and buried, perhaps shallowly. He crawled out of his grave last night. A sentry found him and brought him to us. What could we do? He'd earned the right to die in bed.'

The professor cocked an ear for breath flutterings in the lieutenant's trumpet. He told them, 'They say at the Ogbor he graduated officers' school in July only. Unlucky, eh?'

Moja said, 'He has probably been in Yugoslavia only a week or so.'

'They shouldn't make such babies come, eh?' said Grubich. 'Not for that house-painter bastard.'

'Don't get political, professor. The doctor must be tired.'

She showed him to a room beyond the wards where a camp bed stood near a window without curtains. He missed her company when she went. In no other hospital where he'd ever slept had he felt so strongly that now he was about to lie down with the dying. He thought, I must see if Fielding's ankle is all right. An officer's first duty . . . But behind their partition Fielding and Cleary were asleep. The sober and underfed schoolteacher with the large Irish tough.

That night they all ate large servings of sarma with the professor and Mrs Javich. There was plenty of wine. There would always be plenty of wine in Yugoslavia; blood and wine were, David had already guessed, the national products.

42

The professor talked a lot at table, his English improved
with wine. He said that he would tell Pelham something and
Pelham would not resent being told it, because Pelham and
Fielding were regular guys. They would stand or fall, he said,
by their talent for the tri-arge, the sorting of cases.

When the wounded came, they would come in a crowd.
All the wounds cry out for care, but behind the blood and bone
fragments, some are worse than others and some are beyond
spending time on. When you work alone you must be able to
tell the difference. If you can't, you have chaos, you take too
long to make up your mind, you have your orderlies moving
wounded people first to this bed, then to another end of the
ward, until they haemorrhage. You lose too many, you are
aware you lose too many, you take to drink . . .

Listening, Pelham could not imagine anyone taking to
drink as energetically as the professor had that night. As he
poured his eleventh or twelfth glass, Mrs Javich touched his
wrist like a restraining wife. So, Pelham thought, perhaps
they are lovers.

I have seen, the professor went on, I have seen some of these
apothecaries who practise medicine in our country reduced to
immobility (in fact he used the word *non-movingness*) when faced
with the task of tri-arge. The wounded don't scream here, but
sometimes the doctors do.

Dr Grubich poked a finger at the ceiling and cried mysteri-
ously, 'Be prepared and fight such happenstances in your own
soul, Pelham!'

David did not say that at Force 147 it was presumed that if
you had emerged from the Eton-Harrow-Rugby-Marlborough-
Winchester axis, you'd do well at the tri-arge. Now even in the
mists of wine, he had a second's vision of himself and Fielding
running about hopelessly in a room where there were too
many haemorrhages to be dealt with.

Meanwhile Cleary was flirting with Javich. He turned on the

strutting airs of a parish ladies' man. Pelham could sense some ruthlessness behind the sweet talk. Why had Cleary been demoted twice? One had been too busy with Caroline back in Mola to find out . . .

Mrs Javich looked bored by Cleary's overtures. There was a smile of mere tolerance on her face and blue patches of exhaustion under her eyes. Pelham observed the contrast between her good looks and the lumpy oddments of military clothing she wore. She has fine skin, he thought. But his observation was aesthetic, not sexual.

As was to be expected, Fielding grew quiet in his wine. Sitting back, he seemed to contemplate the state of tipsiness with a mild and courtly pleasure. As a schoolteacher he would have been the type that created his own restrained rituals in the classroom and filled it with a climate of quiet security. Children savoured such atmospheres. If he can do the same for my hospital, I'll be happy.

A little after nine, Moja Javich began yawning frankly. Cleary's honeyed phrases grew a little desperate. 'And I want you always to know,' he orated, 'Mrs Javich love, that when loneliness descends you'll always have a friend, an admirer, an admiring friend, in Charlie Cleary.'

He didn't seem to care if Pelham overheard this ardent speech. All night he had behaved as if he were out of reach of military authority. He could easily end the night by challenging me to a fight, thought David.

'It's time I went,' said Mrs Javich.

'Where, where, love? Where're you going?'

Mrs Javich laughed her high crystalline laugh. 'Do you want a list, Private Cleary?'

'I would treasure it,' raved Cleary. He began singing –

> '*I put neath my pillow each night when I sleep,*
> *The dear little token she gave me to keep* . . .'

44

'Stage Irish!' said Fielding without malice.

'Yes, Madame Javich. An Irishman at the right stage.'

But she patted Cleary quickly on the head and was gone.

The professor said, 'She jump in tub every night, see. Like a film star.' Despite his medical competence, he had a peasant contempt for too much washing.

'Why does everyone mention her name?' Pelham asked. 'Is she a commissar or something?'

'Commissar, no. She got no time for commissar. Why everyone say *Moja, Moja*! is because everyone got special favours from Moja.'

Cleary's nostrils rose. The professor went on.

'Like, she has such contacts. In Yugoslavia. Even in Chetnika. Even, one thinks, in German Army. Like, she finds fleet of convoy trucks – German – last year. The general wants them for this, that – he control part of Montenegro, needs trucks. Moja tells partisans where to go to find trucks. They go. They find. Same with hospital. She set up all what's needed in hospital. It come from German hospital, state hospital here, there.' He dropped his voice to a furry bar-room whisper. 'The partisanka, ordinary partisan, he does anything for Moja. He respect Moja. Why? Like, she's grand lady. Ordinary partisanka – very mixed-up socialist.'

'If she's so valuable, why are they sending her to the coast? With me?'

'Jealous commissar. She piss in commissar eye. Not a political Moja, no, not a political, see. Commissar make a fuss about her. She laughs sometimes at all of them. Commissar make ultimatum. General say, sorry Moja. Go you must. There we are.'

Cleary had stood up and stretched, deceptively relaxed with his weight on the balls of his feet.

'Where are you going, Private Cleary?' Pelham said. Thinking, he brings conflicts with officers to a head very quickly, this Cleary.

'I want to relieve myself, Doctor. All this wine . . .'

'We'll expect you back very soon.'

'I see.' Cleary belched. 'Despite me large bladder capacity?'

'Despite everything.'

Cleary got that nauseated smile which covers great anger.

'You don't mind shaming me in front of strangers.'

'I shall expect you back here and very quickly.'

While Cleary was away, Fielding tactfully excused himself. Then Professor Grubich.

Alone, David looked at his hands, which had gone knotty with angry veins. If that Irish yobbo doesn't come back . . .! Two and a half minutes went. Oh God. He intends to make me go and find him. And very likely he'll insist on fighting, even at this impossible hour. Ah well, one thing can be said for Eton. It is nothing if not a good preparation for dirty fighting in the dark. Yet his hands threatened to begin trembling.

He looked up and Cleary stood in the door. 'Sit down, Cleary.'

Cleary sat sideways in his chair and looked ironic.

'If ever we're friends,' said Pelham, 'you can call me David. Only because we're friends, not because we're refighting 1916. Until then I intend to play things both ways, both as a British officer and a doctor to the partisans. And if you give me trouble, I'll *give* you to the partisans. They have no degrees of punishments and they solve all problems by putting a bullet in the offender.'

Cleary said, 'Talking of punishments. It's been known for men sometimes to punish their officers. In the heat of battle, these things aren't noticed.'

Now good primitive anger had taken over in Pelham. 'Are you offering to shoot me, Cleary?'

'If I was, what would you do? Tell the Juggos?'

'Listen, don't waste your time with threats. Go to your

billet and get your carbine and I'll get mine. And we'll stalk each other up and down this town all the damn night.' Pelham felt, in fact, ready for that sort of enterprise.

Strangely, it was this sort of talk that seemed to pacify Cleary.

'Jesus,' he said, with a new kind of smile, one that had no satiric content. 'You don't know what you're asking for, sir. I'm a commando, you know. British trained.'

There was, in the way he said it, just a margin of compliment for David.

'Why were you demoted, Cleary?'

'You're welcome to look up my record, sir. I'm not ashamed to say it had to do with politics and women.'

'What sort of politics?'

'There's only one sort for my race.'

'Quite. What did you do before the war?'

'I was a dairy farmer, sir. In Clare it was.'

'Why did you enlist? If you're political . . .?'

'It's the only way of getting away from me wife and mother.'

'Cleary, answer me seriously!'

'Sir, I am.'

'You were promoted, twice, to sergeant. Both times it was in the middle of a campaign.'

'Yes, sir.'

'Do you like soldiering?'

'The Panzers were nothing compared to me mother, sir.'

'What fate do you fear most?'

'I don't fear mines, sir, I don't fear high explosives. I fear getting gut-shot. A little.'

'Don't despair, Cleary. You've got me if you're gut-shot.'

'We might call off that little hunting party, sir. The one you were planning for tonight.'

'All right. Go to bed.'

On his way, Cleary turned round. 'Jesus, you're a caution, sir, offering to have me on. In the dark.'

'I don't know . . .'

'You ought to realize. I'm a real killer, sir.'

You could tell by the way he glanced up from beneath his black rustic eyebrows that, of course, it was true.

Pelham began his work in the Jajce clinic by delivering two children of peasant women. The children prospered. They didn't know the violence they were being born into.

Next day a partisan was brought in without a foot – he had lost it in a minefield – and Grubich invited Pelham to trim the injury. Grubich gave the pentothal injection. 'You guys forget Grubich hangs round, eh? Do it the any way you want!' So they did; they managed to forget that this was the professor's hospital, and that the professor was at the patient's head, watching the man's eyelids quiver, taking account of colour and respiration.

Now David had to face, for the second time in his life, the task of amputation. The jagged lower leg had to go. In this, their first test as a surgical partnership, Fielding behaved as expertly as a matron. The artery forceps were to hand, the clips, the bone-rasp, a German brand of bone wax. Whack! went the bone-cutting forceps in the palm of David's hand.

You have to remember to leave a flap of flesh for healing. Otherwise it all has to be done again.

Grubich said nothing throughout. Fielding had the ligatures ready. None of it was a problem.

The same day Pelham met an ancient wound. Four months old. It was a leg hole. The broken bones of tibia and fibula showed dead white in the hole. The sufferer was a middle-aged Serb. His blood count was low, not only because of the wound but because he had walked from western Serbia, living in barns and eating thin soup when he met kindly people.

The wound had never had a chance to heal. Somehow he

48

travelled at night, on many nights. The falls, the inevitable tripping on stones in the darkness, would have brought on fainting and delirium. Misplacing a foot might mean something like scalding agony.

David probed the wound. Its edges were hard as wood. But he could get the bones to unite crookedly. He told Fielding to apply splints. The man should have blood.

David asked the professor. 'Is there enough blood for this man?'

'Plenty of blood. I take as is needed. Even from partisans in the street.'

Early next morning yet another Jajce woman gave birth. So the pattern ran – the births prosaic, the wounds grotesque, the deaths barbarous.

Cleary had arranged with Kallich to go on a reconnaissance patrol. Now that he knew Pelham would not play the paranoid game of rebel private versus bumptious officer, he was happy to absent himself for the day, give the doctor a rest from his presence. For the same reason, David was pleased to see him go.

After bringing Pelham's shaving water, the Irishman clumped out into the half dark streets saying, 'The joys of foreign travel.' He meant it: there was no irony. He saw himself as a tourist.

Towards noon that day Moja and Pelham were both called to the castle. The general stood in an upstairs office. Only an aide was present. 'Moja, Moja!' growled the general, tenderly. Today, Moja, who still wore her brown overall, was interpreter.

The general spoke to her. She listened soberly. It was clear to David from the way they spoke together that they were old friends, and that now and then they made jokes at each other's expense. In the end, Moja turned to David quite formally. He noticed there was an amazing softness in her eyes, but presumed its object was the general and not himself.

However, for the first time in his life it came to him that he might feel a sexual impulse for a woman over forty.

'Do you know the island of Mus?' she asked.

In the background the general muttered, 'Vis and Mus.'

'They are islands on the Dalmatian coast,' Moja told Pelham. 'They are small, but have always been used as Dalmatia's back door. The British Navy used them that way during the troubles with Napoleon. Now the partisans.'

David struggled with memories of Latin classes. Did Mus mean 'fly' or 'mouse'? Either way an image of mould and unhygiene, of sticky wounds and ravenous insects rose in his mind. It would not, in the end, prove to be an inexact one.

The general went on talking. Moja occasionally turned to Pelham, saying such things as, 'He says I am to look after you.' 'He says it is up to me to give you equipment.' 'He says that the partisan knows that should he be wounded he has death or a long hell ahead of him. It is our task to reduce that anguish. We will be the great aid post for all the coast.'

The general lifted a motor-touring atlas from his table and found the page. He thrust it at David, indicating with index finger and thumb two small islands well out in the Adriatic. 'Vis. Mus,' he said.

Pelham thought, does he fight all his campaigns with touring atlases?

Moja, Pelham, and the company of partisan troops would walk south-west from Jajce to the coast. They were to step across the Split highway at night. Trawlers would take them to Mus.

David was permitted two donkeys to carry his equipment to the coast. He could tell that if the general said two donkeys, it was the limit of what the general would supply, that it was wasteful to argue. So he did not argue.

'When are we to go?' he asked.

'Tonight,' said Moja. 'The German Army is moving quickly

to fill the empty spaces left by Italy's surrender. Split has already fallen . . .' (Tito indicated the fact with his thumb and atlas) '. . . and two enemy divisions have begun marching over the mountains from the direction of Montenegro. We have to go at once.'

Tito beamed at him, as if he expected David could not have had better news.

'What about Cleary?' Pelham asked Moja.

'We won't be leaving till midnight. Cleary may be back by then.'

In the evening Grubich arranged a special dinner for Moja, Pelham, Fielding. Outside, in a courtyard of the hospital, donkeys were being laden with contradictory items: ammunition cases, explosive fuses, the surgical pannier, ether in wickerwork bottles, canisters of gauze, lint, plaster of Paris.

The loading of medical stores was the work of two partisan orderlies whom Grubich had given Pelham: one, a quiet little man with a stubbly head called Jovan; the other, a large, lame, wardsman called Peko. This one David had often seen carrying wounded men to and from the operating theatre in his arms.

Meanwhile, at Professor Grubich's table, the raw spirits were drunk. By Moja's side sat a quiet girl of twenty. Her name was Suza. She wore the pants of some foreign army and very large boots. Her eyes had the bruised look of slum children who are brought into a casualty ward with injuries their parents are not willing to explain. She also was to travel with them, as a nurse.

Towards ten Cleary reeled in: after formally knocking, Pelham noticed. Cleary's mother had imposed a strange mixture of manners on him. He laid his sub-machine gun against a chair and took a glass of rakia gratefully.

'Them fellers can walk. And all useless. Nothing seen. I don't think I can eat much,' he said.

He was told he had better. He was told he would march

twenty miles that night. He leaned back in his seat and raised a mute sweaty face to the ceiling.

At midnight they all shook Grubich's hand. Moja hugged him curtly. If they loved each other, they were very monastic about it. And since it was clearly not in Mrs Javich's nature to be monastic, it seemed that in fact there must be nothing between them but warm friendship.

It was as well. They would never see Grubich again.

Chapter 3 Riviera

The partisan infantry who were to travel with them met them by the bridge over the Pliva. At first the party followed the muddy highway towards Travnik. It must have been safe, for there was some chatter and a relaxed air amongst the Yugoslavs.

'You saw nothing of Jajce,' Moja told David. 'You did not see the underground chapel or the execution place of the last King of Bosnia. Most important, you didn't see the Temple of Mithra.'

'I'll have to come back then,' Pelham told her. 'As a tourist.'

'The Temple of Mithra is the place. The cult is so Yugoslavian in spirit. The Roman legionaries brought it here, you know. It's the worship of the bull. When you were initiated, a bull was slaughtered on a grill above your head. You were covered with his blood. His bones were crunched and his bone-marrow poured on you. They believed that from his blood and bone-marrow came the grape and the grain. From his seed came all the animals. There was only life if blood flowed.'

'You don't mean to say it's still practised?'

'Of course not. It died with the coming of Christianity. Yet in other ways it is still with us.'

After a time they took to farm roads, and then to mountain tracks. They moved through sleeping villages and over high hills. David could later remember very little of that four-day journey. It was a haze of rain, cold, deep day-time sleep in pine forests. Even when he closed his eyes he could still see the alert shapes of hiking partisans. On the second night, the scouts met a patrol from the local partisan command. Their news was that the enemy were encamped along the highway, wanting to prevent a breakout by partisans from the direction of the Bosnian mountains. Every few hundred metres east and west of Livno was patrolled by at least a section of German infantry, and forces of company strength were within call.

Standing fast by his donkeys, Pelham could see Georgi, the middle-aged commander of the party, walking down the column, calling softly to this man and that.

'What's going to happen?' Pelham asked Moja.

'He is picking two dozen men to cross the highway first. They'll make a diversion some way from the place we'll cross it.'

'Holy Jesus.'

The two dozen went off. David and the others sat in a ditch for half an hour. They could hear men's boots and German voices.

Then a terrible fury of noise burst out. Georgi began waving his personnel, men, women, donkeys, across the camber of the road, into the fields and foothills on the other side. For a long way they could hear the firing behind them. David presumed that the twenty-four decoys must all be dying there, on the Split highway. Yet every one of the two dozen appeared the next day at the mountain farm where the convoy was resting. Not one had a wound to show. For that Pelham was grateful, thinking of the grains of morphine he would have had to use on the wounded to make tolerable the journey to the coast.

On the third night the moon was up, and they marched on a plateau of harsh grey stone. It was a desert place and cold, and far away they could see the minarets of the lovely town of Mostar.

Moja said, 'The enemy is probably already there, though we don't know. The first arrivals are sometimes killed by the locals. But then others come, and others.'

They marched into the fourth day. In one village, they found Italian soldiers drinking outside a tavern, singing on benches in the sun. New allies, with nothing to do but drink, they cheered the column past, shouting, '*Smrt Fascismu!*', *Death to Fascism*. At the edge of the town an old woman held a portrait of Pavelich, the Ustachi leader, in her arms. She spat at them and cursed them. Georgi laughed. The partisans seemed to respect her for the courage of her sympathies.

At noon they came out of the hills to the little seaport of Podgora. On this morning of steamy sunlight the mountains of the offshore islands were superbly clear, green and blue. All around them the golden beaches shimmered in the wind. There were olive groves and groves of figs. It all looked better than the Riviera. Here, for a little time, Pelham could suspend belief in the enemy-ridden hinterland. He slept soundly all afternoon, in a house in the town.

The waters of the Neretvanski Kanal were the daytime property of torpedo and E-boats of the German Navy. It was only after dinner that night that they could board the trawlers and head south round Hvar and Korčula, the island birthplace of Marco Polo, and so to the port of Grevisa on Mus.

Later, Pelham would often dream of that first approach to Grevisa, still remembering how its black bulk rose, reached out to them and cut off the starlight. From the trawler, Georgi shone a torchlight towards the shore. By its brief light Pelham saw nothing of the dockside of Grevisa, saw only the features of three partisan women seated together near him, atop the deck cargo. The briefness of the light and the way darkness stuck to all the hollows of their faces made them look beautiful and pathetic. He heard the donkeys groaning aft, uneasy at the long swell of the sea. The food bags their handlers had hung about their ears did not distract them from complaining. Georgi turned the flashlight off.

The trawler idled further in. There was no sound ashore for another ninety seconds. Then, from the dock, someone yelled, '*Stoi!*' It sounded to David like the baritone making a monosyllabic entrance in Act II.

Moja stood beside Pelham at the foremast. At the sound of the word, she put a hand on his arm. 'Lie down on the deck, David.' She had dropped by his side and was pulling him down. Her hand was very cold.

In an instant a burst of automatic fire tore the rigging above their heads. Georgi cursed loudly over the gunwales. His voice was high as the firing stopped.

David thought his hearing had been distorted by all the noise. For it seemed that out of the black town of Grevisa someone was yelling in English. In English English. 'Stop that, you stupid bastard!' the voice said. Apparently chastising the gunman.

All at once the dock was there, at Pelham's eye-level. The trawler attached itself fore and aft to bollards above its deck. On shore the futile English voice continued to shout. 'What idiot shone that torch?' No one bothered to answer it.

'Who is that Englishman?' David asked Moja.

'I don't know. Perhaps the British have moved in a few men.'

Georgi's partisans were storming ashore against a boarding party of the partisans of Mus. Forcing against each other like scrimmaging football teams, they seemed to be arguing who was to blame for this ominous landfall.

The Englishman came aboard. David could hear him forcing his way and swearing. Then he must have collided with the donkeys. 'What's on these bloody donkeys? What's this? Wine? The island's full of bloody wine.'

Pelham found the man in the dark. He could dimly see the shape of his beret.

'No, that's ether. And some iodine.'

'Jesus, who sent you?'

In the voice there was some resentment towards unexpected guests.

They introduced each other. The Englishman's name was Major Southey. He said he commanded a troop of commandos on Mus.

'How many commandos in a troop?' Pelham asked.

'Fifty.'

'My God!'

The major called English names in the dark. 'Dewhurst, Brown. Help the captain to unload.'

Soon they all stood on the dock of Grevisa. Cleary whispered at Pelham's shoulder. 'Don't let the major have me, sir. You'll need me in this situation. I'm a good scrounger.'

There was the rattle of a wildly driven truck up the road. Southey said, 'Oh God. Here comes the drunken bastard.' The truck tore madly down the dockside. Yugoslav curses from the scattered partisans marked its passage. It did not halt, and only then violently, until it was on the lip of the gangway. Its driver got down and half ran to Southey and Pelham.

'From Italy?' the driver asked in a firm voice.

'From the mainland,' Southey said. 'You're pissed again, Lawrence.'

'Yes, sir.'

Southey said to Pelham, 'This is Sergeant Lawrence. He runs a sort of debased field ambulance for us. I let him drink only because abstinence makes him ineffective. He should never have been sent here.'

Lawrence stank of spirits. There was defiance in him. His accent was West Country rural. 'We're an independent group, me and my five,' he stated for someone's sake, Pelham's or Southey's.

Pelham introduced Moja and Fielding but left Cleary out, since this was probably Cleary's wish. Southey said, 'We're camped amongst the vineyards up under the mountain. You must come up and visit us when you have time.' But he sounded indifferent.

For a weird reason of his own, some mad chivalry, Southey felt threatened by the sight of a surgical team. In inviting Pelham to visit him, he was also warning Moja and David against settling near him. He told Lawrence to find Pelham's party a place to stay. 'Down here. In the port,' he insisted.

They got into Lawrence's truck, David and Moja in front with Lawrence, the others in the back. Lawrence back-turned, drove rapidly along the dock, scraping bollards as he went. David could dimly see Moja flinch at the noise.

'Go easy, Sergeant,' he told Lawrence.

'It's all right, sir. It's our truck, signed for and all.'

'Your truck and our hides. Go easy.'

Lawrence muttered companionably, 'As you say,' and slowed.

In some corner of the dark he parked and got down, telling them to follow. It may have been exhaustion, but David felt the eyes of watchers on him, and certainly at least two voices challenged them in the dark. '*Stoi. Stoi.*' Lawrence would say, 'It's all right, Trotsky. Engleski.'

Stumbling indoors, Pelham heard Moja crack her head on something in her path. He heard her breath fly from her. 'They've got a bloody gun in here or something,' said Lawrence. Someone spoke in Yugoslav. It became apparent that the front room of the house was taken up by a gun – anti-tank, howitzer? Pelham couldn't tell. It faced out of the wide front window and down the harbour.

Lawrence took them upstairs, closed the blinds, switched a light on. He was seen to be a square dark man, rather short for his heavy bones. He snorted with disgust at the table. A mess of half-consumed tins of beef lay there. They seemed to be decaying, as if they'd been left there suddenly and in fright at least a week before.

'Some of my men,' said Lawrence, 'dregs of the Midlands.' Nonetheless he sat at the table, as did the others. He offered his flask to everyone. The burning rakia was a comfort to David. He watched Lawrence watching Moja drink. The sergeant's eyes widened a little with obvious desire.

David was young enough to feel compelled therefore to re-appraise Moja. All he thought he saw was a handsome lady with hollows of exhaustion in her face. The bedroom Lawrence showed them to smelt clean, like a room where the sun shines all day. But the dark was now so thick, the air like air from a compressor. He felt, as a drag on his chest, the enemy presence in nearby Split.

Chapter 4 Rakia in the Lamps

A sharp point of light fell through the sacking curtain on to his face and woke David. Nearby Fielding slept on his back. Cleary rested beyond Fielding in a ball of blankets. Moja's blankets were empty.

At the window, he lifted the curtain a little. Below and across the street was the bay, theatrically blue, the hills of Mus around it, and not one fishing boat riding there. The blue spine of Korčula seemed close and a small bird hurtled across its hump and came towards Mus at unnatural speed. A mile away, it took on the dimensions of a Messerschmitt. Very low, it traversed the bay and the town. Only when it was gone did David hear the sounds of its engines. Inland, where commandos and partisans lived, there was a rattly exchange of gunfire. Next Pelham saw the plane wheel above the hills at the north end of the bay and roar away to wake the other islands.

Pelham noticed then that Moja was strolling along the dockside. She called up to him.

'A carefree young knight of the Swastika,' she said. 'I've found exactly the place we need.'

Breakfast in Lawrence's mess was properly Anglo-Saxon. An old woman in black, mourning God-knew-what, had cleaned away the bully beef and laid a breakfast of ham and eggs before them. Only the rakia and the black bread were characteristic.

While they ate, Moja and Pelham questioned Lawrence

60

about Mus and its future. He turned out to be a source of more or less exact information. There were twenty-eight enemy divisions in Yugoslavia, said Lawrence. Many of them, of course, needed elsewhere. Now that Italy had surrendered, the intention of the German Command was to destroy the partisan threat forever by a pincer-movement in Dalmatia, and then to take the islands one by one. The island, had strategic value, they should understand. The threat to the islands would come up the Pelgesic peninsula on the mainland. The peninsula was already largely in the enemy's keeping. The vanguard of the threat to Korčula, Hvar, Vis and Mus was the 118th Jaeger Division. Some of the Jaegers had already been taken, questioned, killed by the partisans around Podgora.

The partisan command and allied force headquarters had decided there would be no retreat from Vis and Mus. They had chosen their personnel with an eye to this directive.

'Take Major Southey, for example,' he said. 'I trust that this will not get further, captain. But Southey is a madman. He carries a bow and arrow into battle. He has also been known to carry a claymore. Very tough, but certifiable. And likewise on the other side of the island. There's the port of Mus over there. They've just put a Royal Navy port commander in it and a flotilla of Navy gunboats. All commanded by axe-murderers and lunatics. As a matter of fact, there's a Yugoslav hospital over there as well. Run by a Dr Bersak.'

'Doctor? Tito told me there was no doctor on Mus.'

'Dr Bersak is more like a horse-doctor. I hear he has three sailors there who were injured the night before last. You might want to go and rescue them. I'm sure they'll be grateful for the rest of their lives. I could take you about four this afternoon.'

After their breakfast, Moja led Pelham, Fielding and Cleary towards the stony fortress at the north end of Grevisa harbour. Fielding and Cleary were far enough behind for Moja and Pelham to speak with some privacy.

'That fort there. I remember it from a time – oh, about ten years back – when I holidayed here with my husband. It's a typical Georgian construction. Sturdy. Dry. Exactly suitable for us.'

'Your husband? Is he on the mainland now?'

'No. He's dead of course.' Her eyes swept the harbour as if to indicate the ordinariness of death. 'Don't ask for the story. It's the standard Yugoslav one and you'd get the details mixed up with the stories of other people. And I would like that the death of Marko Javich should not get mixed up with that of other people.' For the first time, David had heard her descend from the most correct English. But there was no tear on her face.

It looked a superb little fort. The stone yellow-grey. Above the main gate GIIIR engraved artfully in the stone. The partisans in the courtyard saluted Mrs Javich energetically. 'They didn't want to let me in at first.'

They passed out of the main barracks square of the fortress, through another gate into a yard. Here stood what Moja had promised. A stone barracks, firm and dry. They walked in the door. Three or four partisans sat on blankets on the stone floor, but the blankets of many others were there, tumbled, matted with mud and rancid to the nose. The men did not look up. They chatted, laughing loudly, intending to convey that they were telling exclusive jokes.

'It has everything,' said Moja. 'At the end there are three storerooms. I imagine we could use them as sterilizing rooms, bandage rooms and so on. Over here on that side . . . come and look.'

She led them into an annexe. It was a little dim but lit by a high glass window. In the middle of the room the pedestal and slab of a table, highly scrubbed.

'It used to be a military hospital during Napoleon's wars,' said Moja. 'When the British were last here . . .'

'This is wonderful.'

62

'There is a cellar. You can see the steps there. You should get it cleaned out. The partisans will do it. Then you can use it to store your blood supplies.'

'A cellar.' He saw the stairs and made for them.

'Best to get the partisans to do it, David!'

As he went down the dark steps he smelt the death smell. He made himself strike a match. The cellar seemed to be full of wine racks, and laid on them, the bodies of people. One of them stared at him but the face was stained with death and carried in it the news of some fatal disorder of the organs. Even for a professional death-dealer, he thought, this is a terrible moment. He climbed the stairs. Moja was waiting for him, frowning.

'A trawler loaded with wounded arrived two days ago from the mainland. Some of them died yesterday and during the night. They intend to bury them today.'

Pelham turned to Cleary. 'You will have to fumigate it after the corpses go. Ask Sergeant Fielding if you don't know how.'

Fielding said, 'You seem to be confident, sir, that we'll talk them into giving it to us.'

'They'll have to.'

'Through here,' said Moja. Beyond the back door of the operating theatre they found a tiny chapel and perhaps thirty tombstones, much eroded. The names were legible. Burrows, said one. Smith, Jamieson, Golder, Baxter, Myles, Whiting, Colman. These sailors had lain here since 1810. 'Across there,' said Moja, 'outside the back gate, there's a large grey house. I looked at it. It seems quite satisfactory for our accommodation and mess.'

'Is there a family there?'

'No, it's been full of partisans. All the families have been sent to Italy by trawler. A lot of the old people have stayed behind as servants. And of course, the young have been wise enough to join the partisans. There's no question that we'll be putting anyone out.'

'Are there partisans in it *now*?' David still felt petulant from his fright in the cellar.

'No, they've been ordered out. You gentlemen might care to examine the house. Excuse me.'

Turning, she disappeared back into the door of that ancient hospital. Instead of going on into their billet, they stayed there and listened to the great Slavic debate that now broke out inside. In the midst of it, Pelham could hear Moja's voice raised to a pitch of shrewishness he would not have expected from that cool lady.

'Maybe I ought to go in there?' Cleary asked.

'I think she'll be all right.'

Five minutes later, Moja returned to the little graveyard.

'There. They're going. The place will need a lot of cleaning. I'll fetch Jovan and Peko.'

Fielding was to oversee the scouring of the fort. He took Cleary with him.

'How in the name of God did you do that?' David asked Moja, while sulky partisans stumped out with their bed-rolls and rifles.

'Persuasion.'

'Come on, Moja. I'm not in the mood for you to be coy.'

'You got a fright in the cellar.' Her hand went to his sleeve again. As usual with her, the touch was both maternal and seductive.

'How did you clear them out?'

'You must not tell anyone, for I may need to use this method again.'

'All right.'

'I told them that a great commissar is coming to Mus next week to set up a civil and military administration here. It is merely the truth. I told them that the commissar was a friend of Tito, and that I in particular am a friend of Tito. I told them that I would inform the commissar that they had all attempted

64

to rape me in a bunch. I told them that the commissar would believe me because I am a grand and educated lady. The price of my silence was that they evacuate the hospital. You see, there are interesting methods available to grand and educated ladies.'

'You ought to be ashamed of yourself,' said Pelham, 'I can't thank you enough.'

The dead, the blankets, the wineskins that had hung on the rafters were carried out by Jovan and Peko. Their owners received them in the barracks square. All that day the store-rooms and main chamber were scrubbed and disinfected. The disinfectant was an unexpected gift from Sergeant Lawrence, who appeared with his field ambulance at mid-morning. Sulphur was burnt in the cellar, and the stink bit into everyone's nostrils. In the grey house beyond the back gate of the fort, Fielding found a dressing-table mirror and suspended it by wires from the roof of the operating theatre.

Towards noon a local commissar entered with a few armed supporters. Grenades blossomed like some quaint ethnic ornamentation down the front of their coats. At first David thought he had come to retrieve the place for his men.

Instead, the commissar began a long speech of welcome, holding his arm wide from his body throughout. Finished, he nodded to a lieutenant, who produced the eternal bottle of Yugoslav spirits.

The toast was poured and Pelham drank a mouthful. It was very raw, and he felt instantly nauseated. Smiling and bowing, he took the bottle from the commissar.

'Fetch the Primuses, Fielding.'

Fielding brought the two Primuses which were gifts from Grubich. From one he took the cap and poured the tank full of rakia. Likewise he filled the little priming cup and lit it. The Primus burnt with a thin blue flame. Fielding chuckled. Pelham smiled, looking up, expecting the commissar to share in his delight at finding fuel. He noticed that Moja was frowning. The commissar bowed curtly and left with his aides.

Moja said, 'I knew he'd get offended. They're so narrow, these people.'

By three o'clock that afternoon the hospital lay bare and clean except for its pathetic fittings: an operating table, a Tilley lamp, a reflecting mirror, two stretchers, a bandage supply, some plaster, a small cache of drugs, two Primuses and a stolen stew pot for sterilizing.

Fielding seemed full of a quiet pride. He and Cleary were then given the task of combing the town for blankets and beds.

In the gold and purple of late afternoon Lawrence and Pelham drove inland. The road rose from Grevisa through an opening in the hills. It was narrow and Lawrence's driving was little better sober than drunk. Where the path hugged the hillside Lawrence braked.

'Look at that,' he said.

From the cabin window Pelham could see not only Korčula and the peninsula but the snowy profile of the Dinaric alps, the island of Hvar, and the whitewashed towns of Hvar and Korčula. 'Not bad, is it?' Lawrence seemed to enjoy pretending that no threat could come out of such a landscape.

Round a further bend, they ran head-on into a strange resonance. Coming towards them down the road were hundreds of armed partisans. They sang a hypnotic, repetitive, blood-stopping chant, the sort of thing you could imagine Zulus singing before battle. Whatever was mad, momentary, insane in man was celebrated in their song.

The contours of the hills drew up the singing and threw it back at them. For a second, David would have given away career, uniform and all, to join them in their ritual drunkenness of song. Lawrence again stopped the truck and the partisans filed past. Lawrence said, 'They're more like bloody savages, aren't they?' but although the urge to join them had passed, David was not nearly as content any more with his Britishness.

In the midst of the line, he saw a small detail of commandos. A frowning young lieutenant, with heavy black moustaches clamped gratuitously on top of his boyishness, led them. The frown on the boy's face interested Pelham. It was not the frown of fear or of self-consciousness. It was more as if all these foreigners, with their noisy singing, were getting in the way of his enjoyment. By some instinct, David was able to decide: that boy is a grim professional, very dangerous to his enemies and perhaps even to us. For he looked as if he were on his way to commit atrocities on the mainland and so to earn future enemy atrocities against the isle of Mus.

'They're going on some raid to the mainland. There's no real need. The enemy isn't even on Hvar yet. But they have an acting military commissar up here who likes to keep them busy. And they don't mind, as you can hear. They're not like normal humans.'

'And that lieutenant we just saw . . .?'

'One of Southey's boys. None of them are normal either. Hand-picked lunatics.'

When the column had passed, they were alone on a high plain with a thin wind. Ahead were vineyards and the heights of Mt Mushtar, tip of the isle of Mus.

Lawrence started the motor again. They drove towards the far side of the natural bowl which was the vine-growing centre of Mus. So, through a further screen of hills, they came down to the harbour. It looked exactly like Grevisa. Perhaps its bay was narrower, but seemed equally ample. There was a fort at the north end.

'That's the sardine factory,' said Lawrence, pointing to a long roof. 'There's one exactly the same in Grevisa.'

'And the hospital?'

'I'll show you.'

They stopped before a building that reminded Pelham of Grubich's hospital in Jajce. The door was open so they walked into a lobby. Straight ahead they could see an operating theatre. They came closer to it, creeping as one does towards something faintly incredible. The table was upholstered with horsehair. That much was visible through its cracked morocco covering. One bare bulb hung above it and could be raised or lowered by a rusty pulley. Near the table, two surgical buckets were placed as if to catch drips from the ceiling. As well, there was a desk with dust and files on it, a piano, and some dispensing cupboards.

Lawrence said, 'Bersak's always been the doctor on Mus. The locals used to swear by him, but they're mainly dead or gone by now. Only the ones he killed are still here, under the turf. Wait till you see the rest.'

Someone behind them said hello. It was a naval officer dressed in the style of *Boys' Own Annual*: roll-neck sweater, webbing belt and revolver, sea boots.

He said his name was Lieutenant-Commander Hugo Peake. He wondered who they were. When told, he was polite and hostile, as Southey had been.

'I suppose you've come to rescue my boys from Bersak?'

'To see what can be done.'

'Nice of you to consult me first.'

'We were going to come and see you,' Lawrence said.

'Listen, don't offend Bersak. He's the only doctor we've had. He doesn't have to take our boys, you know.'

Pelham told the sailor, 'Lawrence assures me we can do better for your men than Bersak can.'

'Perhaps you can. I doubt it. Two of them seem all right. A little feverish. The third is going to die whatever is done for him. Besides, it's a gut wound. You couldn't move him.'

'What happened to them?'

'Oh, they were on one of the torpedo boats. It met with an

68

E-boat on the other side of Hvar. That was the night before last. They were close in and fired at too low an elevation. The shell hit their own railing and fell to the deck, where of course it went off. Comic opera.'

Pelham chose not to smile at this.

'Will you leave the decision . . . about moving them, I mean . . . in my hands?'

'If you insist. Horses for courses, after all. But as I say, don't hurt the old boy.' He turned to leave. At the door he halted. 'Leave a message if you take them. And, of course, I would want to attend any funerals.'

As he went, a man in a loose surgical gown entered the lobby from a cavernous ward on the left. He wore theatre gloves and smoked, an eccentricity which increased his likeness to Groucho Marx. '*Mes chers confrères!*' he roared in French as bad as Groucho's. He ripped off the right glove and pushed his hand at David.

'Wish to see British sailors,' Bersak decided. '*Ici, ici!*'

Leading them into the high-roofed ward, Bersak walked with all the pride of a chief surgeon showing off his work to interns. The three sailors lay in adjoining beds in a ward nearly empty of other patients. David remembered the dead in the cellar at Grevisa and wondered if they would have done better had they been brought here. The first sailor had his arm in plaster. He was a large young man in his middle twenties, and his face was pink. There was a dew of sweat all over his face. At first David believed that here was a broken arm. But Bersak let them know: the man had suffered a shell fragment near the elbow.

'*Grand, grand!*' said Bersak, indicating with his hands that it had been large and jagged. It became clear that there was no padding under the plaster, that after excising the shell fragment, he had sewn the wound up and encased it in plaster. He had not waited to observe if infection threatened the wound, and he had allowed no room in the plaster for swelling. The sweat on the sailor's face became intelligible.

The second sailor had had an identical wound in the leg, and had been treated similarly. Both of them seemed very happy to see Pelham, as if they were aware that, under Bersak, they had their names down for gangrene.

The third was younger, perhaps nineteen. He had not been touched, though he had had some plasma. His features were dismally defined. His body had already opted for death. 'Difficult case, difficult case!' Bersak explained.

'What's his name?'

'Sullivan is his name.'

Pelham bent over the boy. 'Hello, Sullivan,' he said.

The boy had a wound to the abdomen. Bersak had put a dressing over the place where a shell splinter had gone in. Apart from an area of cloth that had been cut away to enable this access to the wound, Sullivan still wore his battle dress.

'That one's going to take a bit of plaster to fix,' said Lawrence. Bersak nodded solemnly.

'My dear Dr Bersak,' Pelham began, 'I can see that these men are in excellent hands. However . . . I am afraid I must insist on removing them to Grevisa. You see . . . I have orders from Italy . . . to attend to all wounded allied servicemen on this island. I would normally be absolutely content to leave them with you . . . but there we are.'

He wondered how much Bersak had understood. He waited for the man to protest. To say, *but you can't move an abdominal wound over those hills*. No such protest however developed. Instead Bersak, *still* wearing one theatre glove, clicked his heels and bowed.

'I understand exactly, my doctor.'

There was something endearing about his goodwill. As long as you didn't have an abdominal wound.

Up to the moment Bersak gave his consent, David had been arguing on the basis that Sullivan would not survive this hospital. What he failed to remember was that he himself was the only alternative cure. Nor how badly Lawrence drove on the hill road. From his small experience in Italy, he knew that abdominal wounds were not moved off the battlefield if it could be avoided. Instead, a few tents were pitched and orderlies and nurses were left there with the stomach wounds, more or less in the place where the patients had got their bullets. He considered asking Bersak for the use of his operating theatre. But its unsterile air and horsehair would be the death of Sullivan. At least you could depend on Fielding to create a sterile theatre.

David hissed at Lawrence. 'Can you drive slowly, really slowly, I mean? Really well?'

'Of course. It isn't my job to mollycoddle passengers. But the wounded, of course . . .'

Lawrence's truck was fitted out as an ambulance, and specially sprung, he claimed, for coping with cases like Sullivan's. Bersak's orderlies loaded the first two sailors aboard, but David insisted that he and Lawrence should carry Sullivan, and only then after he had injected half a grain of morphine into the boy's hand. For once Lawrence drove tentatively in the dark and, after being stopped twice by partisan guards, they rolled down into Grevisa without Sullivan haemorrhaging.

Moja and Fielding met the truck outside the back gate of the fort.

'No half measures,' David told them. 'We're not going to be able to work ourselves into the business. We've got as bad a case as ever we'll get.'

Jovan and Peko, the orderlies Pelham had brought with him from Bosnia, carried the boy inside. They seemed so much more reliable than Bersak's staff.

Inside, everything looked comforting and professional. Someone . . . he had got used to presuming it was Moja . . .

had found a vast infant's cot and placed it in the corner. It was big enough to be ideal for a case such as Sullivan's. The main chamber was lit by a large candelabrum, stocked with long thin tapers . . . another bounty from somewhere.

Pelham was anxious to discover if similar miracles had occurred in the theatre. He found his way in there by torchlight. He saw drums of surgical dressings, properly placed. He saw a Scandinavian-style chrome dumb-waiter, perhaps the pre-war property of a wealthy Mussite. He saw a dresser, looking scrubbed even by torchlight, and a Primus, and a large copper kettle set above it ready to sterilize the mackintosh and the instruments.

Walking out into the light again, he met Moja. 'Moja,' he said, 'where did you get all this wonderful gear?'

'*Where* is a boring subject. If I have to tell you where I get everything, I'll do nothing but talk.'

'Listen, I must eat before I touch that boy. I don't feel like food. But I can't afford to grow faint in the middle of the job.'

'Never mind. Everything's ready to eat at the house. And look who has come back.'

She pointed to a corner of the room where Suza, the partisan nurse, looked sulky.

'I don't know where in God's name she's been. Probably with some girl-friend.'

In the elation of the moment, David turned to her and called, 'Welcome back, Suza.' He had not in fact realized that she had been missing.

The girl smiled. She was very much a Slav. Pretty, with a trace of heaviness about the shoulders and breasts, a promise of middle-aged poundage.

'You have to watch her,' said Moja. 'Every month or so, she wanders away like this. She can be sullen. But the rest of the time she is reliable. Of course she has a story. Like most of us. Come to the house and eat.'

In the bare dining-room, an old woman stood with joined hands by a table draped in white. In the centre of the table stood a vaseful of the last flowers of the year. The old lady bowed. 'This is Magda,' said Moja.

She saw the flowers and advanced on them, lifted them and threw them into the empty fireplace. Immediately she and Magda began arguing in Serbo-Croat. Lawrence winked at Pelham. But David was amazed by this unexplained flower-hatred in Moja.

Sitting, they all ate some beef and drank some white wine. It was arranged there, at the table, that Moja should inject the pentothal. Lawrence offered to surrender his entire stock of plasma to David. It was an hour of absolute urgency, and Pelham could sense in the presence of the others a desire to offer great gifts, as Lawrence had done. Sick in the stomach, he nonetheless forced some beef down. He thought, if I wanted to indulge myself now, I'd begin to shiver.

'He's had a half grain of morphine, Mrs Javich.'

'I understand.'

'Do you know how to make allowances for that when you give the pentothal?'

'Doctor, I'll let you know this simply so that you will be re-assured. My husband was what is called a society doctor. I gave the anaesthetic for his gall-bladder resection on the Queen of Bulgaria. She would have no one else. *She* lived.'

Occasionally, during that meal, Magda would appear at the kitchen door and look at Moja through narrowed eyes. At this sign of conflict, Pelham thought, God help us if we don't save this boy. We'll lose trust in each other. Minor divisions will grow into large ones.

Fielding and Suza went off to prepare the theatre. Half an hour later, Moja injected the pentothal. The Tilley lamp flickered on its fuel of rakia. There had been four sets of surgical clothing in the pannier. They were of old-fashioned cut and rather coarse cloth. In these Pelham, Fielding, Suza and Moja approached their dying patient.

Fielding had left Sullivan in his clothes, because blankets were short. He pulled the trousers down and the shirt and vest upwards. The boy's body was as white as a young woman's. Fielding removed the old dressing with forceps and dropped it in a surgical bucket. The jagged mouth of the belly wound presented itself to them.

Its challenge appalled David. For a second he felt like one of those zany surgeons in comic films. But Fielding was to hand with a swab doused in spirit. David could do nothing but take it and begin to clean the wound and the flesh around it. Then, a surround of boiled mackintosh. Then, a scalpel. Fielding and Suza behaved like experts from St Thomas's or some other surgical paradise. Fielding swabbed, handed ligatures, even cut while David tied off the bleeding points. Before David knew it, the flesh of the wound was clamped back and he had worked up under the boy's diaphragm, opening the muscles. When that was done, he found black blood pooling in the cavity.

Beneath this sputtering light, it would be hard to find where it was coming from. But because Sullivan was young and had no fat, Pelham was able to work the spleen up into the wound. It lay before him like a mushroom, and in it, through a ragged opening, the shell splinter had come to a stop.

Whether the splinter had damaged the kidneys or pancreas would be impossible to find out. David tremulously decided to slit out the spleen. It would not be long work. The problem was that the spleen itself hid the splenetic artery from him. So he had to work blind.

By feel he used a clamp. By feel he tied a ligature. By feel he cut the artery. He heard the spleen splash into a surgical bucket.

He waited for the spurt of blood to run from the cut artery.

He waited for Sullivan's death bleed. It did not happen. His Anglo-Catholic piety rose in him. Jesus, he thought, I thank you for giving me reliable teachers. He had to hesitate before taking the clamp away, for the lamp expired completely for a second or two. When it came up again, he warily released the clamp. No haemorrhage still. He muttered triumphantly behind his mask, 'We'll close the abdomen.'

Half an hour later, Sullivan's pulse was strong. In celebration, Cleary arrived at the hospital with white wine.

The cot was arranged so that Sullivan could be placed in what is called Fowler's position, half-seated, to allow bad blood to run to the pelvis. Everyone believed he would live.

Pelham's surgical team next applied itself to the two sailors with leg and arm wounds. They worked in a gay frame of mind which the two sailors were not quite able to share. David cut away the plaster and the sutures and sprinkled the wounds with sulpha. Fielding and Suza dressed them.

Later in the night the man with the arm wound complained that his hand was paralysed. Pelham had to reopen the wound the next day, and discovered that dear Bersak, in tying off one of the man's blood vessels, had ligatured his funny bone nerve. Now Pelham had no doubts. He was the only doctor on Mus.

With beds which Moja and Fielding pillaged from the households of Grevisa, and others knocked up by Cleary out of sacking and wood, the hospital had somewhere to lay its wounded. But how many wounded? Pelham, Lawrence and Moja debated this.

With his tenting and stretchers, Lawrence could accommodate twenty victims. The hospital, forty at the best. Lawrence said it wouldn't be enough. Even through skirmishes, he said, casualties accumulate. From Mus, twice a week, parties went over to the mainland and returned with a handful of seriously wounded. Each of them would use and, therefore, immobilize a bed for weeks on end. Every night more partisans sailed in from the mainland. Twice a week, new sections of commandos came from Italy. 'I can see nights when we'll need 150 beds,' said Lawrence. David could but look at Moja.

'He's right,' said Moja.

Even the night of Sullivan's operation seemed to confirm what Lawrence believed. Four wounded Yugoslavs arrived. Three men, one woman. For some reason, the Ustachi had cut the woman's ears off. The injury was old, at least weeks old, and bound up with linen which had not been removed since the punishment was inflicted. Two of the men, very young, had bayonet wounds of the same vintage. The fourth had suffered a bullet in the fleshy part of the hip during an excursion to the mainland earlier that month. He too had been hiding, marching, hiding, marching for days. Now, the day after its foundation, Pelham's Grevisa hospital had seven patients and an air of permanency. David sent a message to Southey up on the plateau, asking him to radio stores in Bari for forty stretchers. The answer would come a week later. STRETCHERS REQUIRED KNOWN BATTLEFRONTS NOT REPEAT NOT AVAILABLE YOU.

But Sullivan, that auspicious patient, did well on plasma and saline. His eyes were very bright. He had thin smiles for Suza.

In the house Magda the cook persisted with linen and hardy autumn flowers. A truce came into being between Magda and Moja, the way there are truces in normal families.

On the third day, Lawrence's orderlies moved in a piano which Moja had found somewhere in the town. She fondled its mahogany.

'Still looting?' David asked her.

'This is going to be an open house to all the British on the island. The Yugoslavs can look after themselves. But the

76

British are not good at relaxing.'

'Won't it be noisy? So close to the hospital?'

'The healthy have their rights too. I've already sent a message to Major Southey's commandos.'

'And the sailors on the other side on the island . . . we'd better ask them too.' He foresaw there would be patients to send express to Bari. In that case he would need Peake's goodwill.

At lunch that day they discussed the plasma supply. Lawrence had a small store, all of it now being David's. Bersak too had a small store, but for him plasma came into the realm of fashionable and therefore risky medicine.

'We must set up a blood-donor system,' said David. 'Fielding, do we have a suitable suction device?'

'No. No, sir, we don't.'

'And no refrigeration . . .'

'We have the cellar,' said Moja. 'These cellars are nearly as good as cool rooms. And as for a suction device, I have one.'

'Oh?'

'Binko!' called Moja. The door of the kitchen opened after a while, and an old man with whiskers limped in and took his cap off.

'This is Magda's husband.'

'I see.'

'He's an old Serbian like me.' The old man must have understood, for he laughed and said something in Serbo-Croat. Moja found it funny.

'What did he say?'

'Please.'

'Come on, Mrs Javich.'

'He says Serbians are known for the size of their . . . equipment. He says Magda only married him for that.'

They all laughed a little at Binko's nationalist witticism.

Moja said, 'What we should do is find a stock of wine bottles.

We should sterilize them, Binko can use rubber tubing and syringe to start the flow of blood going from the donor's arm into the bottle. When the bottle is full we remove it to the cellar. All the bottles can have sterile caps so that the only non-sterile part of the process is Binko's oral contact with the tubing. In the circumstances, a small risk.'

Everyone laughed far more at this scheme than at Binko's joke. It contrasted weirdly with the polite hospitals in which they had all been trained. It made them uneasy. Yet at the same time, it seemed a piece of triumphant improvisation, and the very thing they must now try.

'He'll have to shave his top lip,' Moja said. 'He'll do it if I ask.'

And so he did. Cleary was the first donor. His pint would probably go off before it would need to be used, but it was more in the manner of a symbolic donation.

That same afternoon, Lawrence and David drove up to the central plain to speak to the commissar Pelham had offended two days before. It seemed that the gates of Britannic bounty were opening, and the armed trawlers from Italy were bringing equipment to the partisans. Who were very literal, Lawrence said, and would not give up anything to the British on Mus unless it was specifically marked for them. Amongst the commissar's stores were six large tents which David hoped to take and pitch, during blood-baths, on the slope behind the house.

Today the commissar was friendly: it seemed that an insult to rakia was not a lasting one. But he kept saying again and again, 'These tents were given to the partisans.'

'I am here to look after the partisans,' Pelham told him.

'It is very kind of you,' the commissar said through his interpreter. 'But these tents are for the partisan army.' In the end David could see that in this man's skimping mind, the wounded were no longer partisans.

After the interview, Lawrence told David, 'You should have brought the missus, sir.'

A fortnight later, Pelham had the tents in any case. One night when the armed trawler, *Rake's Progress*, entered the port of Mus, Cleary, Fielding and Lawrence raided the cargo and came back to Grevisa with hundreds of ammunition boots, items beyond value in leather-starved Yugoslavia. Cleary was drunk with the triumph of avoiding the hair-trigger Yugoslav guards. David could see that a career of petty crime under the threat of great danger would suit Cleary for the rest of his life.

'How was it they didn't hear you?' Pelham asked him.

'We walked about in our socks, sir. Bloody cold.'

In the end Pelham was able to drive back to the commissar's headquarters and exchange him a third of the boots for the tents. The rest were kept in reserve as a means of doing future business with the authorities.

Nights were often busy. One night the partisan raiders came back and, with them, the two sections of commandos and their frowning lieutenant. In the bustle of tending the wounded, new working schedules came into being. The hiatus was over.

That night, for the first time in his career, Pelham had to extract an eye. More than that, an eye embedded with a sliver of steel.

Fielding bridged all David's hesitations. First he helped apply the speculum, forcing the eyelids apart. He turned the screw to fix the lids obscenely wide and show the whole face of the damaged eye, the steel sliver biting deep into the iris and white muscles. Again David found the right instrument for each step slapped into his hand. The retractor, the forceps, the strabismus hook, the spoon, the needle holder.

Pelham repaired the socket as well as he could and packed it with sterile cotton wool soaked in boracic. So that the man

79

might one day be able to roll his glass eye comically for his children.

Most of the wounds were from shell fragments. Working on them, David realized he liked this unorthodox surgery as much as Cleary liked unorthodox soldiering. You didn't falter in your decision as much as you would in a proper hospital. You knew that nobody, not even yourself, maybe not even Bersak, could harm these wounded as much as their wounds did.

The commandos had carried their sergeant-major ashore and brought him to the hospital. He had been shot in the chest. It was a complicated wound. It did not bleed much or call out to be immediately explored. But soon it would need a better hospital than Pelham's.

Pelham went to talk to the young lieutenant. He found him leaning by the door, rubbing his beard in a contemplative way.

'Hello, I'm Pelham.'

'I know. I'm Greenway.'

'I wondered, has Major Southey made arrangements for serious cases to be shipped back to Bari?'

'I suppose so,' Greenway said without expression.

David repressed the urge to ask where Greenway had been these three or four days past and what his sleep had been like amongst the enemy.

'You look tired,' he said instead. 'What were your casualties?'

'The sar-major and the ones you have. And we left three behind. Two were missing and one was beyond it.'

'Dying?'

'He had this hole in his chest. You could fit your fist in. There wasn't any use bringing him.'

'The sergeant-major, he has to go to Bari.'

'Okay. Let's hope the *bora* doesn't get him.'

The *bora* was the local north wind of which everyone talked. Pelham had not yet felt it.

'Did it do any good, this excursion?'

'We took the movement orders and files of a German battalion. I imagine that's good enough.'

So the sergeant-major was readied to be shipped to Bari.

At dawn, David understood with some amazement that he had not yet lost a patient.

Into the harbour of Mus several nights later came even the man Greenway had left behind. He was a tall leathery man of thirty called Blair. When left for dead, he decided to crawl towards the rendezvous beach during periods of consciousness. There, amongst the hummocks, he lived for three days on rain water and his emergency rations. In the end the partisan ferry-men found him.

Faced with Blair, Pelham explored the injury, applied ligatures to the bleeding points, filled the wound with sulpha; then labelled him for Bari too.

The pattern of life on Mus was set. In the mornings they shaved and loosed a fusillade of small-arms fire at the morning Messerschmitt. Even Pelham kept a service revolver by the wash trough for the purpose. By day, Binko sucked as required; Cleary scrounged, and flirted with sombre Suza; Moja bullied and requisitioned her way across the island; Lawrence parked his truck in the sun and drank; Pelham held a morning out-patients' session to which hardly anyone came except a few refugee women in transit. By night, he operated.

In Moja's mess the commando officers, growing weekly in number, sang and boozed. Many nights, David was free to sit amongst them and listen to their astounding talk. Some of them were by no means a film-maker's concept of the ideal British combat officer. 'A lot of our chaps are pansies, you know,' one of them told him. 'The War Office knows it. That the right kind of pansy is the bravest of all in battle.' Others, such as Greenway, had a tight-lipped schizoid quality to them. Pelham guessed that they were men who would never get over warring. From people like them the Black and Tans had been recruited.

Those who were not homosexual were always looking for some handsome partisan lady whom they could secretly cosset. There was endless talk about what to say to the woman, where to take her, and if caught, what to tell the commissars' court.

Southey would drawl at them from his corner by the piano, 'If you bastards are found aboard a partisanka, there's nothing I can do for you. Twelve inches from *Mons Veneris*, you leave the benign territory of King's regulations and come under partisan law. General Alexander himself says so.'

Whenever Moja was present they would say charming drunken things to her. She accepted it all very willingly, she seemed to expand even on the stalest, most boozy, endearments. Such moments reminded Pelham of her femininity. He resented her for it, though he couldn't say why.

Sometimes they would hear at night the exchange of fire between British and enemy ships. Allied bombers groaned eastward above their heads, making for the Rumanian oilfields and German Central Europe. When he heard them Pelham thought, maybe we won't die. Maybe the enemy will be stung by tonight's squadrons so sharply that he'll turn away from us. The trouble was Ploesti was so far from Mus, and the enemy coast so visible.

Out in the straits the fishermen of Lasovo and Korčula flashed their shrimp lights. No one attacked them. Everyone liked their shrimps too much.

After two weeks of its rakia diet, the Tilley lamp threatened to flicker out altogether. Lawrence made the eternal boozer's joke. 'If it does that to a Tilley lamp, imagine what it does to me.'

Cleary promised to steal methylated spirits from the *Rake's Progress* next time she berthed in the dark at Mus. In the meantime, he said, what about that generator up at the commissar's? No one knew which generator. Cleary told them. The one under the outside stairs at the commissar's quarters on the central plateau. The commissar wasn't using it, Cleary told them. He lived and worked by candlelight.

Pelham suggested, 'Perhaps he does that because the generator's beyond repair.'

'Give him some boots for it,' Cleary urged. 'You ought to see some of the generators I've got going on farms in Ireland. I've brought light to more Irishmen than Jesus himself.'

The next day, after some solemn trading, the generator and a half dozen bulbs were put on Lawrence's truck and brought down to Grevisa. Cleary begged or stole wire from the signals unit. Before touching the rusty generator, he wired the theatre and the main ward. This Celtic back-to-frontness disquieted Lawrence, a more literal man.

For days, while the rakia lantern paused and stuttered, Cleary cleaned and repaired the motor. For days he frowned over the coil. The others had begun to presume that he would be involved in some Gaelic despair with the mechanism for the rest of the war. At least it would keep him from trouble – Cleary was the sort of man of whom you think: he must be kept from trouble.

Just the same he was not able to get Lawrence's orderlies to help him carry it into a storeroom. They would not take part in such madness. Only Jovan and Peko, of a mad race themselves, would give him a hand. He took some petrol from Lawrence to prime the motor.

'Don't fill the tank,' Pelham told him. 'In case there's a misfortune, so to speak.'

In fact David wondered whether the storeroom would explode. Cleary could tell this. He fell into a deep silent anger. His hands pressed the machinery emphatically. At last he spoke to David.

'Sir, I suppose if some other bastard did it you wouldn't be so afraid. Because poor bloody Cleary spends weeks fixing the thing you expect it to kill everyone.'

'Very well. Go ahead. Fill the bloody tank for all I care.'

All about the ward were the switches and sockets Cleary had manufactured. The switches were nails stuck in metal slots. There must have been some dangerous farms in County Clare.

When the motor started, everyone was about. Some to laugh, others to take Cleary by the shoulder and tell him it didn't matter. Cleary adjusted the throttle and, as gracefully and gradually as lights in a theatre, the six lights of Pelham's hospital came on. David found himself weeping privately. Moja more obviously.

They stood about amongst the wounded, who were also laughing, or trying to! They drank a toast to Cleary and the machine, and Cleary (for his own reasons) baptized the thing 'Deborah', using some of the wine.

Moja said, 'There's no reason why we can't light the house.'

'It'd be a simple thing, a simple thing,' sang Cleary.

He was drunk with their fraternal feeling for him. David thought, all at once we're like a family. What a lucky thing. He looked up and saw Suza's wide, brooding eyes on him. Lately, he realized, she had often stood back like this, dwelling on him. She had some terrible history . . . father eviscerated, brothers and sisters shot . . . something like that. As Moja had said, one got the stories mixed in Yugoslavia.

Meanwhile, Cleary kept making wild joyous noises. It was obvious he had rarely had such a good day in all his life. He had more than he had hoped for: respect, a life of stimulating danger. He had Moja as mother and sister, and somewhere, David was sure, he had a Yugoslav girl.

In the midst of the boozing in the ward, the generator raised its humming to a roar and all the lights dazzled like the sun and then exploded. Though it was day, Cleary stumbled like a blind man to the side of the machine. Its throttle had broken. From now on, whenever they wanted light, someone would have to stand by the generator, holding the throttle with a spanner. 'Oh Jesus, oh Jesus!' Cleary kept saying.

But where it mattered, on the operating table, there would be light.

They found, however, there were no more electric lamps on the island. It was not until the *Rake's Progress* next came into the port of Mus that they were able to trade a goat for lamps. The goat had been procured by Moja. David could see why commissars might resent her. Private ownership of goats was prohibited on Mus. All creatures on the hoof, all meat and milk, were subject to the commands of the commissars. To their doctrinaire power she opposed the quaint and vanishing power of breeding and background. No doubt that was why men such as Rankin spoke of her with warmth.

Whenever Cleary had leave he would go off with a fishing line and camp on the beaches to the north-west of Mus. After a few days he always came back with fish, but his pallor suggested that, as well as fishing, he had done some riotous drinking and, perhaps, riotous womanizing as well.

In Cleary's absence, Lawrence let you know how much he detested Irishmen.

'My dad employed them in the depression. In the orchard. Cheap labour. Even so, he never got value out of them. Like you don't out of Cleary.'

'I don't know. We got the generator . . .'

'That's all. And that was one of those Irish mysteries.'

'And you have to remember the supplies he pilfers for us.'

'It suits him. He's a bloody brigand. But you try to get him to do anything reliable . . .'

'Didn't he lift some lint the other night?'

'Yes. They hid it in Hugo Peake's office.'

'Weren't you going to bring it over here yesterday?'

'I'll get round to it. This afternoon. Or tomorrow maybe . . .'

Lawrence went on holding Cleary responsible for the feck-lessness of Irish apple-pickers in the depression. While he himself drank too much and failed to deliver the lint.

David knew how close the man was to collapse. How necessary the booze was. Since it fuelled Lawrence, it fuelled their one truck.

Moja was sick one day when a case of accidental wounding came in. Therefore David went up to the mess looking for Suza.

'She's gone for the day,' Lawrence told him.

'But there's an anaesthetic to be given.'

'I can do that.'

Pelham hesitated and a silence grew. 'You stick to the truck,' Pelham said at last. He could see Lawrence's hurt in the colour of the forehead, in the corners of the mouth. 'Thanks just the same.'

He would have to anaesthetize and operate both. But that was better than putting a pentothal syringe in Lawrence's hand.

As Pelham left the mess, Lawrence called out after him.

'Captain.'

'Yes.'

'When they land . . . when the slaughter's on . . . you'll be as big a mess as me.'

Pelham decided to be conciliatory. 'I think you could bet on that.'

It was so close to winter, yet Magda still found vivid flowers for the mess. They looked like jonquils but could not have been. Most of the time Moja let them be, but one day as she sat down to her soup her eyes fixed on them. She began spooning her

86

soup but the jonquils spoiled it for her. In the end her old ways overcame her. She got up, grabbed the bunch by the stems and, as once before, threw them into the fire.

'Flowers?' she asked. 'Advance guards from the 93rd Division have landed on Brač.'

'You're sure?'

'The commissars have just been told.' She settled again to her soup.

For the first time Pelham understood she was afraid. As badly as Lawrence or himself. And flowers unkindly reminded her of the springs she mightn't see.

'Don't worry,' she muttered as the jonquils fried. 'Vis will hold. And Mus too.'

But Lawrence, further down the table, fancied himself as a home strategist. 'Mrs Javich, you know that isn't true.'

The sap of the year's last blooms candied in the fire and filled the room with a strange threatening sweetness. That night Pelham suffered a sweating nightmare of a hospital where all the linen was foul; the wounded screamed on the table, wide awake in spite of any amount of pentothal; the floor of the operating theatre lay beneath bloodied swabs and cut-out organs, and rust sat on all the instruments.

Chapter 5 Christmas in the Madhouse

A member of the committee of commissars often visited out-patients at Pelham's hospital. She was a tall woman, very thin. Her nose bone looked as sharp as a knife. She was a pharmacist.

'They call her Propaganda,' Moja whispered to Pelham. 'She sees to the morality of the girls. She is a witch-hunter.'

Somehow Commissar Propaganda had got a stock of Vitamin D and every few days, she came to the hospital and required Moja to give her an injection of it. She would thrust a phial at Moja, growling, 'Feel weak, feel weak'. It was Moja's plan to switch the precious liquid with water. But, in the manner of hypochondriacs, Propaganda had keen eyes.

Another patient was a twenty-five-year-old girl, very dark, with crippling stomach pains. Cleary was detailed to steal bismuth for her from the supplies landed for Bersak by the *Rake's Progress*. Her name was Anka. She was not built to carry a short Italian rifle into battle against the Jaeger Division. Yet she had done it and seen terrible skirmishes.

Pelham found that the girl suffered amenorrhoea – a lack of normal menstruation. He spoke to Moja about this strange condition.

'I know,' Moja told him. 'They all come to me. There are hundreds of the poor things on this island, you know. Hundreds of partisan women bearing arms. They all suffer from it. Some of them think they're pregnant, others that they're witches. In neither case are they right.'

Sometimes he wondered if he should write to the BMA about it: The hundreds of women carrying weapons on Mus who did not bleed. Savage and not caressing, killing and not begetting.

Sometimes Propaganda was at the hospital at the same time as Anka, the girl with the stomach pains and no periods. The lady commissar watched her narrowly out of the corners of her eyes. It seemed to Pelham that some jealousy was building there, in Propaganda's lanky and uncherished womanhood. Maybe she suspected Anka of a happy love affair. Maybe it was Anka's beauty Propaganda could not tolerate.

One cold morning, Lawrence and Cleary were driving back from a night raid on the partisan supplies in the port of Mus. On the plateau, the morning fighter caught them. They sheltered by the tyres of their truck. Tracers shattered their windscreen, tore the upholstery, ripped the canopy, splintered the bodywork.

When the plane flew away Lawrence stood up irritable from fear, from having shared danger with the Irishman.

While they inspected the engine, they heard a wailing close by. They knew it was a Yugoslav woman and though they could not see her, they thought she had been wounded nearby during the raid. Then, amongst the vineyards, they saw a group of partisans. It was from them the oddly musical keening rose.

Lawrence and Cleary rushed towards the wail and found a dozen armed partisans, some of them women, faces set, loosely encircling a place where two women stood digging their graves. These two were the ones who made the terrible music. They were already waist deep in the holes they had dug amongst the gravel. Their senses were stretched wide, they were aware of the noise of the visitors' boots before any of the execution squad were. They looked up out of their twin graves, hissing. At the sight of the uniforms and the faces from the hospital, they showed a second of mad hope. Both Cleary and Lawrence saw that one of the women was Anka, who twice a week brought her unhappy stomach to Pelham's outpatients'. Her face was already smeared with clay. It gave her a ritual look.

Cleary and Lawrence understood that they were seeing that instant partisan justice of which they had heard so much.

A man in charge told Anka and her twin victim to stop digging. He forced them out of their graves with flourishes of his machine-carbine. Their wailing rose in pitch. Their boots slid on the gravel. The faces of the dozen executioners were shut down like Sunday shops.

'Hey!' Cleary yelled.

No one took notice. He walked into the circle.

'Hey, listen . . .' Lawrence had also walked forward, but to drag Cleary away. 'You stupid Mick, you stupid Mick!' Lawrence kept saying.

Some of the squad cocked their weapons and came forward, calling threats. For the first time you could see that they had summoned together enough cruelty as was needed to last them until Anka and her colleague were shot. They had not bargained on having to find extra to last them through interruptions from British soldiers. Therefore, they were desperate to get rid of Cleary and Lawrence. To do it, they would even fire on them.

'Come on, we'll get Moja,' said Lawrence. 'Moja's the only one . . .'

'Bloody barbarians!' Cleary roared at the executioners. But the mention of Moja brought his reason back. He and Lawrence began to run for their truck. They would speed down to Grevisa and bring Moja back to save the girls. As Lawrence sat forward reaching for his ignition key, they heard a short volley of shots cut the moaning off. In the sharp morning air they could see members of the squad dragging the victims' boots off, stripping the bodies. Cleary leant out of the cabin and vomited. Lawrence drove slowly home. As if he were reluctant to carry such news.

Moja began enquiring around Grevisa concerning the charges on which the girls had been shot. Even she could not discover much about commissars' courts. She told David that it was believed the second girl had gonorrhoea, a disease which brought sentence of death.

'A pretty radical treatment for clap,' David said. Though he did not feel flippant about either of the deaths.

Anka herself, so the rumours went, had been indicted on evidence brought by the apothecary Propaganda. The evidence seemed to have been a combination of moral and political charges. It was said that Propaganda had quoted Anka's visits to Pelham as evidence of pregnancy.

The next day Propaganda came to the hospital for her shot of Vitamin D. David saw her in the doorway and dragged Moja with him. Together they blocked her way.

'I want you to tell this woman,' said Pelham, 'that she is not to come to my hospital any more.'

Moja would not translate however. She argued with him. 'A doctor can't take that attitude.'

'Do you think I'd be reported to the BMA?'

'She's a very powerful woman.'

'I thought *you* were the grand and educated lady. I thought you weren't afraid of commissars.'

He watched Moja's upper lip go pink. 'To hell with you!' she told him.

'I want you to tell this lady that when the enemy comes and her brains are hanging out of her forehead or her viscera on the floor, I shall not touch her.'

Moja squinted at him. It was a look of queenly contempt. 'Do you think I wasn't going to speak to her? And in a way of my own? More potent than anything an English youth could manage.'

'As long as she doesn't appear here again.' He did his best to turn away with dignity.

Later he saw Moja and Propaganda in the churchyard. Propaganda was crumpled over the tombstone of one of the long-dead British sailors. Moja stood above her like Medusa. You could hear Propaganda choking and sobbing.

Occasionally Moja made a guttural noise of contempt like stones rolling together. Propaganda emitted the weird feline hissing Yugoslav women favoured. Unexpectedly, David saw Propaganda too as some sort of victim. If anyone loved her enough, they might put a bullet in her as well and lay her by Anka in the cold side of Mushtar.

In the misty mornings of December you could still sometimes see the snowy peaks of the mainland and, closer in, the white towns and beaches of hilly offshore islands. Even in winter it was the stuff of travel brochures. Yet that month the islands were falling. On Brač the Luftwaffe began using the airport. There were Wehrmacht units in every town on Hvar. The islanders offered little frontal resistance, but learnt once more (as they'd been learning for some centuries) that enemy soldiers under threat of irregular attack, of murderous ambush and skilled acts of terror, are themselves likely to be unkind.

As the islands fell Southey and the partisans sent out nightly raids. The raiders had got so adept that they brought back few casualties. For a few weeks most of Pelham's patients were the fruit of enemy reprisals.

Notably, Pelham treated an eighteen-month-old boy child with a bullet in his hip. Though he could soothe the screams with dangerous doses of narcotics and remove the bullet, there was nothing he could do for the fragmented bone.

Moja looked down on the child blankly, unsurprised.

Without the pawkiness and good humour that usually lit her face, she began to look merely pretty and almost as drawn as you might expect of a tired woman of forty.

'Who would do this?' he asked Moja.

Moja stared at him a second. She could not believe the naïvety of the question. She said gently, 'Frightened boys. Obeying frightened officers.'

'Those commandos up on the plateau. Some of them are frightened. But they'd never do this.'

'Just because you know their human faces you think they can't be inhuman? The boys who did this had faces. Besides, it might have been an accident.'

'You mean they might have been aiming at the mother and missed?'

'Don't be ironic.' She smiled and looked small, girlish and golden again. 'Anyhow, I'll show you something they did mean. Those boys with faces.'

She led him to the end of the ward where Fielding was tagging new patients. A thin boy wearing nothing but a shirt lay on a rubber draw-sheet. His crutch was a gangrenous stew.

'How old?' Pelham asked.

'Thirteen,' said Moja. 'He's from Korčula. They questioned him about his father and his uncles. He wouldn't or couldn't tell them. They suspended him by his genitals in a well.'

David probed the boy's stomach but could not get answers from him concerning either pain or numbness. In the end, a silent hunched eunuch, he was shipped by trawler to Bari.

Ten days before Christmas Pelham came from the hospital and found a rowdy party in the mess. Only Lawrence drank quietly. Everyone else seemed to be shouting and finding what was shouted funny.

'Starting Christmas early?' Pelham asked Lawrence.

'No. Just toasting Greenway.'

David saw Greenway and remembered the evening the young man had marched poker-faced across the plateau with the chanting partisans. Greenway now sat in the best chair, smiling . . . smiling a sparse smile while others asked him questions and laughed.

'Why Greenway?'

'Because he's a Christ-Almighty killer? What other reason? The brave celebrate him. So too the not-so-brave.'

Giving Lawrence up, Pelham pushed into the group around Greenway.

'Here's the cutter,' Greenway said, seeing him.

'What's happening?'

A commando officer leaned in. 'More a question of what *has* happened. Tell him, Greenway.'

'I've already been through it half a dozen times.'

'Tell us again. It's a real tonic . . .'

Greenway sighed. He looked at David as if he could sense in the surgeon a core of mistrust.

'Well, it began with a prisoner we took. Don't know what happened to the poor sod, but while he was with us he told us a Wehrmacht entertainment troupe was going to visit Korčula. Friend Southey thought an entertainment troupe would put the bastards at their ease, make them relax. So . . .'

He told how at night he crossed to Korčula by trawler, climbed through the olive woods to the ridge above the town, and took advice from the partisans hiding there. They gave him peasant clothes to put on: a sheepskin cap, a fur-lined jacket, baggy pants.

On the evening of the concert he loaded his Sten gun on to a donkey. Two partisans travelled with him to the edge of Korčula and promised to wait. He could hear the beer-hall music rolling from amplifiers throughout the town. The occupying power was out to prove that it was at its ease. The sentries at the walls were not polite but seemed content enough. As if they could not possibly die within sound of comic songs of home.

Greenway knew how to find the back stairs to the commandant's billet. It was a good villa in the Serbian style. He knifed the sentry, mounted the stairs, knocked on the door, felled the housekeeper who opened, knocked on a door behind which the German broadcast from Radio Belgrade was playing. The door was opened by the regimental commander, said to be a solitary man. On a desk on the far side of the room Greenway could see files and other office material. Instead of listening to comedians, the colonel had been working late. Greenway shot him through the head. The amplified songs rolled on. No one came. Greenway collected all the files and documents that were in the room, roped them together, took them downstairs to his donkey. He slung them across the donkey's neck and covered them with a blanket. So, while the band played, he found his way out through the ancient walls and up into the black forests.

There was a silence when Greenway finished. Pelham was at the centre of it. Everyone watched him. Then the listeners around him began laughing, a deep painful belly laugh. You could see the German colonel's nightmarish death made them feel somehow they wouldn't die nightmarish deaths themselves. As if that season's roster of bizarre injuries had been filled up and, therefore, they themselves would not appear on it. So Greenway's story was already becoming a fable they would suck on all Christmas.

Someone said, 'And the papers he brought back!'

'Important?' Pelham asked.

Greenway shrugged.

'Code books, movement orders,' one of the officers said. 'Isn't that so?'

But Greenway sat still, staring cannily at Pelham. You know (the eyes said), we all know. The files are just routine office stuff. But they want to pretend otherwise.

Later, as David left the mess, Lawrence put a hand out to stop him.

'What I wonder,' Lawrence muttered, 'is how many poor sodding Korčulans'll get shot as reprisals? And what kind of torture cases the trawlers'll bring in? And what the bloody Jaegers'll do to us when they get here?'

David said nothing. He felt cold in the wrists and the small of his spine.

Lawrence went on. 'See. The hero's a fucking murderer.'

'Dear Caroline,' Pelham wrote for the girl at Mola. 'These Adriatic mornings are lovely. I wish I were here as a tourist. Even so, on mornings like this it's possible to believe *they* will never come here. Given the sort of personnel we have here, if ever they *do* come it will be a ferocious battle . . .'

He looked up from his writing desk in the bandage room. Greenway, a bad colour, stood in the door.

'Can I do anything?'

'I can't sleep. Is there something I can take?'

'I can't spare much. Not on any long-term basis.'

'My insomnia won't be long-term. Just till Boxing Day.'

'I don't understand.'

'The old bastard comes that day. General Greenway. Who begot me some time back. A one-day inspection of Mus. Boxing Day.'

Greenway's mouth stood open. The breathing was heavy. Panic attack. It often overcame people before meetings with hated parents.

'I can give you four phenobarbs. Take one tonight. If you still feel bad take two. You see, I can't spare more. There's the wounded . . .'

'I understand.'

'The feeling you have . . . It'll go away.'

'Thanks. Anyhow the old bastard might drown before Boxing Day. It happened to Lord Kitchener.'

General Greenway came into Mus by torpedo boat in the small hours of Boxing Day. The commandos he inspected in the early morning were sent out after breakfast to search for his son, who had disappeared overnight.

At noon a runner fetched Pelham from Grevisa up to Southey's headquarters on the plateau. In Southey's office a small bristly general waited for David.

'This son of mine,' the general said, not introducing himself. 'Has he spoken to you, Captain?'

'He asked me for sleeping tablets, that's all. He seemed just a little overwrought.'

'You gave him tablets?' The way the general said it, it was a serious accusation.

'Yes, sir.'

'Enough for him to do anything silly with?'

'Just four half-grains of phenobarb.'

'A soldier should use grog. There's no shortage of grog, is there?'

'I think phenobarb was better. In this case.'

'You act as his psychiatrist, do you?'

'Not exactly.'

'Nonetheless . . . When you see him enquire of him why he wants to embarrass me in this manner. Tell him I'd prefer a frontal attack with weapons than this kind of snide attack.'

'I'll say you said so, sir. I don't think it will help.'

'Tell him this. I know he's a physical coward. Now Southey wants him given the Military Medal. Because he killed some bloody colonel on Korčula. That's like giving a blind man a certificate that says he can see. No bloody use at all. And ask him this. Ask him what sort of man can't face his father? Ask him that.'

'I don't think they're the sort of questions a doctor should ask.' Pelham thought, I'll be arrested. Because my anger, my contempt, must be obvious to the general.

But the general merely snorted. 'Do you think the main job of an army doctor is to give cowards sleeping tablets? The main task of an army doctor is to *thwart* cowards.'

'I'm not really an army doctor, sir. I'm an irregular. Under the authority of the Foreign Office.'

'Get out! You're like *him*!'

Chapter 6 New Year

Perhaps Mus was to the theatres of war what an appendix is to the human body. Strange and intractable elements found their way to Mus and flourished there. In December Southey was made a colonel, in January a brigadier. Fast flourishing!

Another Mus oddity was the major who commanded a squad of US engineers on the plateau. Early in the year these men began to beat out a landing strip beneath Mushtar. Now there was some chance that disabled planes could manage a landing on the island.

The major was a professional Texan and wore his service revolver in a cut-away holster on which stood a metal star. Some of his men were brought to Pelham suffering alcoholic poisoning. The Texan waited soulfully on the hospital threshold for word of them. To him alcoholic poisoning was an honest wound.

In January too a seventy-nine-year-old innocent, bent on a glorious death, landed from the *Rake's Progress*. He was a rear-admiral no one would employ in saner places. His name was Sir Martin Harris.

David met him on a cold morning in the new year. They had left the hospital to Fielding, and Cleary had promised to show him a beach where the monks had taken miraculous draughts of fish in the Middle Ages. Cleary had had more normal success there.

On the way to his day's fishing David stopped at the port of Mus to speak to Hugo Peake, the port commander. They sat and talked in the winter sunlight outside Peake's office. Further down the mole, Pelham saw, an old man was strolling in a much-braided naval uniform and sea boots. David watched the old man come nearer.

But before Pelham could ask who it was, a lazy burring noise filled the air. Looking up, he saw lean-bellied dive-bombers rise over a seaward spur of Mushtar, gaining height before falling on the town.

Hugo Peake stood up. He yelled to the old man down the quay. 'Down, Admiral, down!' It sounded like a man ordering his dog around.

Far from dropping, the Admiral raised a hand slowly to his brow. Like a land owner watching ducks circle in season, he watched the bombers come in for their run.

Pelham and the others lay down against their wall; their mouths were close to the mossy place where the stonework met the paving of dockside, hiding their breath from the enemy. Against the thin whine of the bombers Pelham could hear the old man yelling improbable things – 'Bastards!' and 'Save your breath!' and, after the first bomb had come shrieking in and exploded down the quayside, 'They wouldn't feed you in the RAF.'

'He's mad,' Hugo Peake called for David's information And the ground shook. David felt soft clods of something, maybe turf, landing on his head and clothing. A second later, he was aware that the clods were oily, and a little of the oil ran into the corner of his mouth. 'Sardines,' he said. 'They've blown up the sardine factory.' He began to laugh.

On their second run, they hit the foyer of Bersak's hospital, doing damage to masonry. Soon Bersak, in his everlasting coat and surgical gloves, would begin moving shattered stonework away from the doorway of his hospital.

New Year

After the bombers had turned home, the untouched Admiral came jogging down the pier towards Peake's office. You could tell from the way he ran that, alongside his other madnesses, he was a compulsive long-distance runner. He ran straight into the office without speaking to anyone.

Hugo Peake said, 'If I'm like that when I'm his age, I hope someone will shoot me.'

'Where does he come from?'

'He landed one night. He's too old for a regular navy job. In North Africa he used to drive around the desert with an Indian tank regiment. He was captured but the Germans gave him back. I can understand their point.'

'Gave him back?'

'Yes. They gave him back. Then they broadcast over Radio Berlin that they weren't interested in 78-year-old Admirals. The silly old bastard felt shamed by that. That's the point, he doesn't hate the Germans on political grounds. I'm sure he and Hitler have a lot in common. But he hates them because they considered he was beneath the normal usages of war.'

They watched the smoke fuming from the sardine factory. Already the town smelt exclusively of fragmented sardines.

Hugo Peake suggested, 'I say, Pelham. Would you consider certifying him?'

'On what grounds?'

'Well, you just saw him.'

'I'm sure *that* doesn't qualify as madness with army psychiatrists. Only with normal people.'

'There are other things,' Peake said. 'The other night he bullied me into letting him go out with one of my patrol boats. They ran across the beam of a regular little fleet of E-boats and Siebel ferries. They cut the motors and waited for the enemy to go their way. But the Admiral immediately took command of the ship and grabbed a megaphone. *Ram the bastards!* he yelled. Happily my boy talked him out of it. They gave him tea laced with narcotic. But there you have it, lunacy.'

The Admiral called from the office. 'Peake, are you coming? Paper work, my son! Paper work!'

Peake whispered to Pelham. 'He tells me that after he's set my office to rights, he's going to go up to the plateau and help Southey out. I hope Southey lets him go on raids.'

Pelham spent most of his fishing day helping Bersak clear the entrance to the Mus hospital. As they bent together and strained at stones, he could smell the gangrenous stench from the wards. His own hospital stank by the standards of respectable medicine, but Bersak's reeked like something from another century. David thought, with that smell in their nostrils, no wonder Europeans were once a religious race. That stink is a homily on the contingency of man, on the impossibility of living forever.

Suddenly he wanted to educate Bersak. As tactfully as it could be done.

'I was reading the other day,' he said, leaning on a crowbar, 'how badly wounds in the limbs used to be treated. I mean, as recently as 1918 the treatment was primitive. The article said it was only during the Spanish Civil War that new methods came in.'

'*La Guerre Espagnole*,' Bersak muttered without intonation.

'Yes. That's why I'm interested to observe your use of plaster of Paris . . .'

'Oh yes. *La gypse . . . toujours la gypse . . .*'

'You may have heard of Trueta, the Spanish war surgeon. He found that in fact treatment of jagged wounds in the field worked best with dressings, wool paddings and plaster over the top.'

'Oh yes, Trueta. My guiding star.'

'Of course the wound swells and stinks but slowly gets better.'

'I see it happen. Here.'

'The essential thing is the padding, allowing the wound to expand.'

'Padding.'

'Yes.'

'Here there is not much padding.'

'Trueta, your . . . guiding star, believed that the plaster was not good on its own.'

Pelham wondered if Bersak would grow offended. But the doctor smiled.

'We must all make do, eh? Make do from what we have.'

'Indeed. It doesn't work with hand wounds, I believe. One should not immobilize a hand injury in plaster. They say you should get the hand moving as quickly as possible. Of course, I know about these matters largely in theory. I often wonder if experienced surgeons – such as yourself – find the theory is helpful . . .'

'Maybe. But here there is always room for the experiments.'

'It is always good to speak to a veteran,' said David. You could see the crystalline brightness of unquenchable ignorance in Bersak's eyes. David abandoned the debate and threw his weight into levering stones out of Bersak's doorway.

Pelham and Moja Javich became lovers over the question of a German airman.

One cold night in mid-winter Southey's men and the partisans landed on Hvar and struck the little port of Jelsa. For some reason, they brought back a number of prisoners, even some wounded German officers.

These men were laid in the corners and by the threshold of Pelham's hospital, they had no priority for treatment. Orderlies stepped over them, attending to commandos and partisans, who had priority.

Pelham could remember wondering that night whether such

preferential treatment was moral. Perhaps everyone who took part in a war was damned, because the obvious things to do in war were all barbarous and inhuman.

He did not have much time to debate this question. There was a young commando private who had gone up to a German strong point to accept its surrender. Close in, he had been cut open by machine-gun fire. Lawrence sent him in first to be operated on, although it was all beyond hope. Yet there was an aura of outrage about the returning raiders which passed itself on to Pelham's team. It made them accept, without thinking twice, that this boy was to be first on the table.

The pine surface must have seen the astonishing butchery of Georgian naval surgeons. And now the work of Pelham, tending the commando's bleeding points, cutting out seven feet of riddled intestine. Then he sewed up the useless vitals. Meanwhile, German officers died quietly under the orderlies' feet.

By the time all partisans and commandos had been tended, most of the enemy's wounded had died. Lawrence's orderlies slipped on the flaccid limbs and swore. They found a young Luftwaffe pilot alive with a mere leg wound. He was clearly a dandy; his hair was arduously arranged and was still in good order despite the battle, the wound, the sea journey. In shock he was talkative, especially to Moja. Even as she prepared the pentothal injection, he chatted away, his head turned towards her.

'What's he saying?' Pelham asked.

He noticed then in Moja and glum Suza a special unsmiling quality. David felt the quality of another, primal age in the room. In the judgement of these two women the boy was forfeit.

Moja injected the pentothal and the boy slept. Pelham treated him according to Trueta, the Spaniard. It all happened automatically; David's head was light, floating high above the bloody port of Grevisa.

Before the end however he ran out of made-up plaster. Fielding was outside, taken up with the chores of after-care. Suza, for a Yugoslav, did not make good plasters. Pelham looked at Moja.

'I have to make up a plaster. Don't touch the boy till I get back.'

Suza's eyes and Moja's eyes threatened him above the rims of their masks. He thought for a second, my God, they'll dismember him while I'm gone. In the manner of some ancient Illyrian sacrifice.

Moja spoke through her mask. 'What do you mean?' she said. 'You despicable boy!'

He made a slight shrug in a way that was meant to say, I don't want to discuss meanings after a night like this.

'Then I am finished with this man.' Moja's fingers began working madly at untying the knots of her theatre mask.

'For Christ's sake, Moja, stay there till I get back.'

He walked out. The main chamber was a clutter of improvised beds. Wine bottles with saline drip or blood sucked the day before by Magda's toothless husband, hung inverted over nearly every bed. Where there were no stands to hold the bottles upright, partisans or commando privates held them in grimy hands and yawned.

All this improvisation did not amuse him tonight. If Lawrence died or deserted, if Fielding went, the system would come crashing down. Again his stomach seized up with the question: What would happen the night the Germans landed on Mus?

He walked down the aisle which Fielding had skilfully managed to maintain amongst the dying. At the door of the storeroom a dead German officer sat. His eyes were open. His face seemed both grimy and transparent. He looked unspeakably tired and David could see the haemorrhage that ended his life encrusting the front of his jacket. Worst of all, he sat there with an air of ownership, so that Pelham would have to hurdle him to get to the medical stores.

David found himself shouting, 'Who put this bloody corpse here?'

Two of Lawrence's orderlies appeared at his side.

'See if you can find an *intelligent* place to put him.'

After they had begun lifting that knowing corpse away, Pelham understood the unfairness of talking like that to men who all night had exercised their own skills as well as he had exercised his.

This was the one sign he gave all night of being frightened and doubtful about his resources. He made the plaster, and went back to the theatre. The work was finished in silence.

'Thank you,' he said at the end. Moja did not answer. Neither did Suza. Not that Suza ever said much.

He had three hours sleep. In daylight, the hospital looked more professional. He found many sturdy pulses amongst the wounded. And the boy with the stomach wound was beyond pain, in his final coma.

Later in the day he was aware that Suza's brooding eyes had gone. 'Where's Suza?' he asked Fielding.

Fielding's eyes avoided him. 'The commissars sent for her.'

'Commissars?' He remembered Anka.

'Yes. Sir, you'll have to forgive me. That girl's infatuated with you. Not in a healthy way.'

'My God. They think that she and I . . .'

'Yes, sir. Whereas . . .'

'Whereas?'

'Nothing, sir.'

You could see that Fielding was no gossiper, that he was one of those reputable northerners with no conspicuous need of women, drink, or gossip.

'Come on, Fielding. Don't treat me like a maiden aunt.'

'Whereas she has been making do in the meantime, so to

speak, with one of Lawrence's orderlies . . .'

'That's nice. Lawrence's orderly impregnates her, and she and I get shot for it.'

'Should I tell the man you want to see him, sir?'

'Yes. And before nightfall.'

Only then did he remember his debt to Fielding. 'And I want to thank you, Sergeant.'

'Sir?'

'For your help last night.'

'There's no need to thank me.'

My God, Pelham thought, he's so old-fashioned in ways. David had a sudden, maybe light-headed desire to know more about the man. Light-headedly, he gave in to it.

'How do you vote, Fielding?' he asked.

'I . . . I don't know you have a right to ask that, sir.'

'Do you think I'd use it against you?'

'I'm a Socialist, sir.'

'Like Tito?'

'There are times in human affairs when only the extreme means work. Tito works. Mikhailevich doesn't. Perhaps Mikhailevich is a better gentleman. But that isn't the question.'

Fielding did not apologize for his little political homily.

'I want to see Suza's boy-friend.'

'Sir.'

Since David could not leave the hospital himself, he sent the stretcher bearer Jovan out looking for news of Suza. Meanwhile, he made another round of the wounded. By chance, he came to the German pilot's bed at the same time as Moja. The boy's breathing was shallow, his sleep deep. He had reacted strongly to the pentothal.

Moja stared at Pelham. Accuse me! her eyes said.

'It sometimes,' David muttered, 'takes twenty-four hours for them to wake up.'

'I am aware.'

At mid-afternoon, Jovan presented Suza to him. 'Commissars,' whispered Jovan, shaking his head.

Suza had been weeping. Her cheeks were stained with it.

'What did they say to you, Suza?'

But Suza could only speak German and Serbo-Croat.

'Mrs Javich, Mrs Javich!' David called. Moja presented herself. She joined her small hands in front of her apron, like a proper matron, as if to chide him for using the formal *Mrs Javich*. 'Would you please find out where Suza has been and what has happened.'

Moja took the girl into one of the storerooms and at last came out. 'She's been at the commissars' house up near the mountain. They have been interrogating her.'

'What about?'

'About her relationship with you. I would be very careful if I were you.'

'You sound indifferent.'

'It would be sad to lose your talents, that's all.'

'Moja, I don't for a moment believe you gave that man a fatal dose of pentothal.'

'I should hope not.'

'I wonder is it Propaganda again? Doing this to Suza?'

'I have already considered that question,' said Moja, still indifferent, still professional. 'If I find it to be so, I shall have her removed from the island.'

'Oh?'

'Yes. Oh.'

Outside a whey-faced orderly with curly brown hair waited for him.

'Sergeant Fielding sent me, sir.'

'Are you Suza's friend?'

The orderly blushed in a peculiar way. He loves her, Pelham saw. Perhaps he sees me as the ultimate rival.

'Listen, the commissars think it's me. Do you understand,

108

they think it's me. I'm not going to die for you, son. You'll be under arrest up at Brigadier Southey's camp. The brigadier will oblige by drawing up all the proper papers. Go and wait in the storeroom.'

The orderly began to obey but waited in the doorway. He was perhaps eight years younger than Pelham. He had the underdeveloped jaw that went with growing up on a bad diet in the twenties and thirties. Here's a love story for you, thought Pelham. Poor lost Suza and the kink-haired orderly.

'Sir,' the orderly said, 'if it's . . .' He shrugged. 'It won't happen again.'

Pelham thought, Moja says she'll get rid of Propaganda. Why not see if she can?

Nonetheless he continued harsh.

'How can I accept that?'

'The poor kid isn't going to last much longer, sir. Sometimes she doesn't talk for days.'

'Listen, you've halfway contributed to my getting a bullet. Don't give me instructions.'

The orderly hung his head. His mouth was open.

'I was just trying to tell you the truth of things, sir. I'm at your mercy. I know that.' The orderly grovelled, because twenty years of experience had taught him grovelling was best. Pelham felt sudden disgust for himself and for the British way of things.

'All right. Get out. But if you go near her again I'll have your balls on a platter. Lawrence will watch you, Fielding will watch you, I'll watch you.'

'Thank you, sir.' The orderly saluted and went back to the tents behind the mess. In them still lay the overflow of last night's wounded.

In the main chamber, the German airman had still not woken up. Moja went about the hospital, maintaining the air of a Clytemnestra. She did not speak to Pelham again until late that evening, when he was eating soup in Magda's kitchen. She came in and dropped a tag by Pelham's plate. It was the sort of label they tied round the wrists of patients being sent to Bari.

'Would you please sign it, doctor.'

Tabes Dorsalis said the tag.

'Tertiary syphilis?' said Pelham, interpreting the tag.

'That's right' said Moja.

'Who has tertiary syphilis?'

'Commissar Propaganda came this evening begging for an injection of Vitamin D. I gave her pentothal. She is in the back of Sergeant Lawrence's truck. We intend to ship her to Italy.'

'But she hasn't tertiary syphilis.'

'No one will know that until she is in Italy.'

'There'll be trouble. With the committee of commissars.'

'They don't know what *Tabes Dorsalis* is. If they did they might shoot her. I've already written to them, assuring them Propaganda needs treatment in Italy. They haven't asked too many questions. Perhaps they too want to be quit of the poor wretch.'

He signed the tag with his clearest signature. 'Moja, this is wonderful.'

Moja did not smile. 'I suggest you write a letter to Commander Peake, asking that she be put on the first trawler. If a trawler is not available, a motor torpedo boat should make a special journey.'

Calling for paper, he wrote the letter. He noticed that he began many words with the wrong syllables. The letter was full of crossings-out. The loops of the 'H's' and 'L's' were badly controlled and the 'N's' at the ends of words were nearly beyond his power to write. He finished the sheet of paper and gave it to Moja. 'The German boy is still not awake,' she told him.

He had little sleep that night: there were so many small emergencies – delirious risings, broken sutures, descents into coma – amongst the wounded. The large crises looked after themselves: four men died of internal haemorrhages.

But in the morning the Luftwaffe pilot was conscious. He still talked a lot, calling across the ward to a fellow German who had lost an arm.

Pelham asked Moja, 'What is he saying?'

'Small talk,' she said dismissively.

'Please.'

'He says that when he saw that Slav bitch come up to him with the anaesthetic needle, he thought his time had come. He also says that he bombed hell out of Split. He says it was easy, there was no flak.'

'He's only an overgrown boy,' David said.

Moja looked him full in the eyes There was a combined contempt there, for himself and the young pilot. As if they were brother-products of the same unsuitable generation.

At mid-afternoon, when he entered the main ward again, there was a crowd of armed partisans round the beds of the two German survivors. They extracted the German pilot from his bed. They did not handle him roughly, but you could not doubt he was going to his execution. His eyes were wide and childlike.

'You can't move my patient,' said Pelham.

One of the partisans turned to soothe him. '*Nov, nov,*' said the partisan. '*Pokret. Smrt Fascismu.*' Though he spoke gently, a half dozen of the abductors cocked their weapons and held the orderlies off. So the two Germans were kidnapped.

Immediately the partisans withdrew, David ran for Lawrence's truck. Sleeplessness and inexperience made his journey up to Brigadier Southey's camp a wild one. On the way he came close to colliding with the column of partisans and the two wounded Germans slung across the backs of donkeys.

Southey's billet was a presbytery on the plateau. On its steps, David pushed sentries out of the way. He gained the brigadier's office. The peninsula, the mainland, the islands which Southey plagued were displayed on a highly-coloured map above the brigadier's desk.

Southey himself sat writing on a services airletter form. The handwriting was small; it was a packed, newsy letter.

'Hello, Pelham. How's the Juggery?' Juggery was his whimsical name for David's partisan hospital.

To his own surprise, David found himself invading Southey's side of the desk, leaning over the elegant little man. He said, 'I have to show those bloody commissars they can't go lumping their Marxism up and down my wards.'

'You seem very upset, David.'

'It's got nothing to do with my being upset.'

David told him about the invasion of the wards.

'You want me to take the men out of the partisans' hands?'

'Of course.'

'And what do I do with the bastards, David?'

'Send them to Bari. By night.'

The brigadier covered the letter with a file from his in-tray. In doing so, he seemed to renounce the private Southey. 'No,' he said. 'And it's no use arguing about it.'

'Then why?'

'All right. Between you and me. Don't tell those other sods.' He seemed to mean his junior officers. 'I have unofficial advice, but from a high source. To let the partisans have all German prisoners. No one in Italy wants me to send any back. Of course they can't say so much in a written order. If I shoot prisoners, I wouldn't put it past them to try me as a war criminal when the fighting stops. So, I simply give them to the partisans. I don't suppose you've ever heard dim firing from the direction of Pegosa?' (Pegosa was a tiny island half a mile south-west of Grevisa.) 'It's not very noticeable amongst the general racket. However, that's where the partisans execute their prisoners.'

He sat down again and uncovered the letter. His mind was

half on the next sentence as he spoke. 'And why not? The other side do the same thing, and will do it to us if ever they land. Only mention it to you so you can make your arrangements. You know what I mean. Have two bullets ready. One for the bastard who breaks in the door, one for yourself. If you prefer cyanide tablets I have a supply. But more style ending yourself with a pistol. More appropriate to a soldier.'

Pelham thought, why did I bother appealing to him? Perhaps because he seemed sane while drunk in Moja's mess.

The brigadier said, 'Listen, must turf you out now, old chap. There's no call for depression, mind. However, I'm afraid you'll have to let the commissars into your hospital whenever they want to come. You may have noticed, it's their island.'

Driving home, David's heart began to thud. Sweat ran over his body and the tingling sensation of fainting was in the tips of his fingers. It occurred to him that he was in hell, that there was no one around him who was not a monster. When he parked the car he could not force himself back to the hospital, but went instead into Magda's kitchen. He felt grateful that it was empty. He poured himself a large measure of spirit from one of the kitchen's many bottles. Booze, booze, booze, he thought. Mus – temporary branch of hell but a boozer's paradise.

The rakia brought him a physical warmth, that was all. In fact, a weird telepathic terror rose in him. He had no doubt it was the same terror that existed that second in the German pilot with the leg wound. He thought, as directly as the German boy was thinking it at the time, he thought, leg wound! How can I run from the bullet with a leg wound?

He heard the stove creaking in its mid-afternoon rest. He heard a floorboard creak as well. Next he was aware Moja stood at his elbow.

He accused her. 'You approve of all this.'

'Who said so, David?'

'When you gave him the pentothal. You knew it was going to happen.'

'Yes.'

'You bitch, Moja!'

Moja picked up his glass of rakia and threw it into his face. The spirit burnt his eyes, but he tried not to show it. Shaking his head, he tried to jolt his vision back into seeing clearly.

Moja had gone, but only as far as the door.

'I would rather not be here,' she said. 'I would rather be living off other people on my estate. But no one permits it. History doesn't permit it. History is on the side of the commissars.'

Pelham still winced from the burning liquor. 'We have to go and see these bloody commissars, Moja. You and me.'

'And what are they to do with prisoners, eh? You took a veritable rope ladder of guts out of an Englishman last night. He's dead now. But that doesn't distress you. This pilot distresses you.'

David, still probing tenderly the corners of his eyes, tried to frame words. The taking of the German threatened him and the hospital. He had lost the British commando on the surgical merits of the case. He had lost the German because the fragile circle of his professional care was invaded by men with automatic weapons. And because it might happen again at any time, the diabolic wounds he had treated yesterday and must treat again tomorrow had become all the more intolerable for him to remember or touch.

Of course, he began weeping. He couldn't wait for the woman to leave.

It was such a blinding release of tears that all his senses were drowned. A minute passed before he understood that Moja was somehow kneeling by him, caressing his head against her shoulder.

'Go to hell,' he said.

'Why?'

'I won't have you damn well mothering me.'

She said, 'I won't mother you. There's a promise.'

She began massaging the inside of his leg, about three inches above the knee. With a hunger that reached back into his brain, his body accepted the hand.

Moja said, 'I know I am older than you . . .'

He said nothing. He was intent on fitting his mouth to hers.

She helped him upstairs to her bedroom. If Magda saw them, she never said anything. David could have, in any case, passed as sick. The sexual comfort of being helped along by Moja had loosened all his muscles.

When she took off her drab clothes, the Italian army pants, the asexual partisan smock, she showed a body startlingly young and fine-textured. 'Oh God!' said David.

Chapter 7 The Affair

From then on Moja avoided the mess on the nights Pelham was there. Perhaps she thought the atmosphere of the place might betray her into giving some sign of their very happy love affair. Apart from that, she did not change her manner. The air of pervasive motherhood she carried about with her prevented everyone but David from seeing her as an individual more or less in love.

He found it hard to believe that the bounty of Moja's body had been given to him, of all the men of Mus. That small body that reminded him of peaches. For the golden down on her arms and at the small of her back gave her the look of something freshly ripe, of girlhood that had never worn off.

When they lay together, satisfied, Moja seemed, without effort, to radiate warmth to every corner of the room. At such times Pelham felt, we're so innocent and lovable lying here. Perhaps even the Jaegers will see that.

Before sleeping they did not talk much about the past. She gossiped; he commented. She knew so much about everyone on the island that she was able to tell him things about his own staff he didn't know.

The reason Lawrence drank so much was that his wife had given birth to a child. The child had been born last November, fifteen months after Lawrence left home. Lawrence was a farmer, she pointed out. It was hard for people who lived in farming communities to tolerate these things. It was hard for

Lawrence to live it down. If you're a city dweller, these scandals get dispersed, she said. But amongst farmers a man is marked by such scandals for life.

Then she showed him some of the weekly poems Cleary solemnly addressed to her. *The Rose of Mus,* one of them was entitled.

> 'They call her the rose of Mus.
> Her beauty is half of the cause,
> And with wounded men
> She does what she can,
> Her touch is as soft as a puss.'

David and Moja writhed about the bed, hooting. You must promise never to say, she told him.

When he reacted to such stories, her hands darted over his body and her fingertips pressed into his flesh. She seemed to be imparting to him by these means that he mustn't laugh too loudly, but that the story was all for him. A gift.

Did he know, she went on, that Cleary had recently had a conquest with Suza, who was a lost, easily-seduced girl? She had spoken to Cleary and warned him off.

Did he know that Fielding was a monk by temperament, a true partisan? Already the man knew his Serbo-Croat and spent his free time translating the Kosovo, Serbian heroic songs, into English. 'As long as he doesn't rhyme Mus with puss,' said David.

The story made him remember a night when they had all been in the mess, Fielding, Lawrence, Pelham, at the hour a squadron of enemy bombers struck Grevisa. The bombers seemed to be aiming for some target in the upper part of the town. Therefore the hospital and mess were safe. The noise was nonetheless dizzying.

Most of the visitors lay on the floor for safety or crouched behind armchairs. Magda scuttered in from the kitchen and threw herself down beside a bulky partisan officer. Between explosions, Pelham could hear the piano playing wildly and loudly. At first he thought it was a symptom of ear damage. Looking up he saw two partisan girls crouching by the piano and, seated at it, Fielding, pounding out Kolo dance music. Fielding, who would more appropriately have thumped out the *Internationale* in some dusty church hall, now made sweet drunken music.

The partisan officers heard it and got to their feet. They grinned and grabbed for Magda. They formed with her a loose circle. The partisan girls joined them. Then a few of Southey's officers. Within twenty seconds the room was pounding with dancers. The partisans laughed at the inexpert steps the British took. The muscles and blood of life pulsed in the music.

Invasion was expected by mid-February. Everyone seemed to regard that coming date as a date without any crucial meaning – like the day when tax returns have to be sent in. He did not know if inwardly they felt the same panic he did. He didn't know if he could stand being put against a wall, the last surface he would ever experience, if he could last the seconds till the bullet arrived without whimpering and urinating. It wasn't that he just wanted to die with dignity. Surgery and the practice of medicine taught you that people die only with varying grades of indignity. He didn't want to die at all.

Now the question of death was complicated by Moja, in that the Germans would probably kill the two of them in the same instant, and his ravings and beggings would be for her too. Was it possible, even as he made love to her, that in the pocket of her Italian army overalls, she had some instrument of suicide?

'Oh yes,' she admitted one night, 'I have a cyanide capsule.'

He ran his hand down her arm and inspected the neat elbow. He couldn't imagine her dead. He couldn't imagine the blue eyes put out, quenched.

'If I got forged papers for you . . . I could talk to Southey about it. We could make you a nurse in the British Army . . .'

'Nurses in the British Army will be shot too. I understand the enemy. They know what would happen to them if *they* were taken prisoner.'

He closed his eyes.

'What?' she asked. 'What is it?' She rubbed his left ear as if to release an answer from him.

'Moja. Give me the capsule.'

'Why?'

'Let's make a pact. You and I. When they come, we'll be together. Probably in surgery. Let's take our chances with the firing squad.'

'I'd probably forget the damn thing anyhow,' Moja said, shrugging sweetly, nakedly, abandoning recourse to the capsule.

Pelham said, 'It's easier to believe in the Virgin Birth than in you and I becoming so much meat . . .'

Applying three fingers firmly to his lips, Moja prevented him from completing the sentence.

The second week of February was the worst for Pelham. At night the threat seemed close, lying in the mist just beyond the window panes, a condition of the climate. He wondered how other men could sleep in their black rooms, behind the black-out curtains, without Moja to make the dark habitable.

He resented the fact that all sleep and all love was by courtesy of the German High Command who could crush Mus any night they chose. To Pelham they were a terrible divinity and their power was absolute.

On the Sunday night that ended that week he waited in

Moja's room for her arrival. It was ten o'clock. He had sat in the mess a while, but few soldiers were there and no Yugoslavs. It seemed everyone was close to his battle station.

There had, however, been little work for Pelham to do that night. By shipping some people to Italy by trawler and discharging others, he had almost depopulated the hospital. He could not even pass time by chatting with Magda and Binko. They took to their bed about nine. It was a massive old brass structure, a hundred years old, and they seemed to be confident they could hold it against the Jaegers or the Edelweiss Division.

At last he heard the truck brake outside the hospital. An orderly had driven Moja up to the plateau to visit some refugees and now she was back. When she came in and held him her clothing was cold. Her vivid eyes were abnormally alight, but at first he thought it was just because she had come in out of the cold and found him waiting.

'Wonderful news,' she said. 'Wonderful news. The commissars are letting it out, tomorrow it will be all over the island.'

'What?' he said. 'What news?'

'The partisans from the island of Vis raided a port across on Brač. Sutivan, the port of Sutivan. They captured some papers that showed the German High Command set next week for the invasion of Mus and Vis, dependent on weather. Well, now they've postponed it till the third week of March.'

Pelham could not speak. He began whimpering with the relief. 'Oh Jesus,' he managed at last. 'Is it true?'

'Of course.'

'It's a lifetime.'

'The raiding did it. The raiding by the commissars and Southey.' She kissed him as she spoke, wide-mouthed kisses on the forehead and jaw. 'I know you don't like Southey. But he keeps us alive.'

'Jesus,' said Pelham. 'A month. A lifetime.'

120

'The news is better than that. Tito needs places to retreat to, namely Vis and Mus. You see, the allies have chosen Tito. So they'll bomb the mainland bases and the Royal Navy will bombard them and sink their supply ships. The allies haven't written us off. That's what it means, darling David.'

'Oh,' he said. 'Oh Jesus, Moja!' He bit her neck.

'If they've got the power to make the German High Command delay for a month . . .'

'Then they've got the power to make them postpone for two months!'

'Three months!' said Moja.

That night, for the first time, Pelham made love to Moja in celebration and not as a gesture in the face of death.

The stay of sentence filled everyone on Mus with a mad optimism. Southey and the commissars planned more nuisance raids.

'I threw my cyanide in the latrine,' Moja confided to David. But she could tell that this gesture had not exorcized David's fear, which now fixed itself on the new date in March.

'Well, Moja. How do you like loving a coward?' he asked her.

She rubbed her thighs against him energetically. Their flesh too seemed golden, as if she had spent the past years in the sun, not in the daytime warrens and night time marches of a guerrilla war.

'No,' she said. 'You're sensible to be frightened. It's all still in balance.'

'Then why did you throw away your capsule?'

'Didn't you ask me to?'

The population of the island used the good news as cause for a minor winter carnival. The mess was full and there was singing, dancing and drinking in the ports and under Mushtar. Into these revels fell Callaghan, his Hurricane fighter landing on the plateau strip prepared by American engineers. Escorting bombers towards Rumania, it had had an oil tank punctured by tracer. The tank had not burned, but he had glided down to Mus, his motor croaking, a thin trail of black smoke behind him. Landing, he buckled his wheel-housing. His seat moved forward on its mountings and crushed his ankle against the wall of the cockpit. If it had not been for these two minor accidents he might have taken off again after small repairs, and so retained his innocence.

He was an Australian. Solid and dark. He had that endearing callowness that comes with growing up far from the European mess.

David had to strap his ankle. After being lectured by Southey about women, he was welcomed to Moja's mess. For a twenty-two-year old, he showed himself to be an accomplished drinker.

When liquored, he would climb on a chair beside the piano and sing songs of the bush. You could tell he was convinced he was bringing culture to the northern hemisphere. With what he had seen of Europe, perhaps he had the right to believe that.

His songs worked superbly in the mess. Even the partisans liked *We camped at lazy Harry's, Flash Jack from Gundagai, The Old Bullock Dray*. In the same spirit, Callaghan paraded his native dialect.

Later in the week, when it was time for the *Rake's Progress* to return him to Italy, Callaghan claimed he had slipped on the mess steps. He was too lame, he said to go back on duty. Besides, he said as well, he felt *crook in the guts, he could have shat through the eye of a needle.*

Pelham inspected him. 'I feel too crook to travel,' Callaghan kept saying. David could not do anything but believe the patient.

'Ripper!' Callaghan said. 'Fuckin' marvellous.'

Half an hour later, David saw him in the mess. He was leaning over the back of the piano, listening to a lady partisan playing contemplative songs. There was a long tumbler of *procek* in his hand. Seeing David, he did a comic hobble half way across the room. He held up the glass of thick, fruity liquor.

'Great stuff for the Joe Britts,' he told Pelham. Joe Britts was Callaghan's rhyming slang for diarrhoea.

Pelham said, 'I hadn't known.'

Callaghan sat down beside him. 'Fair go, doctor. This is a real holiday for me. It beats Italy. Sure as hell, it beats the Mallacoota branch of the State Savings Bank of Victoria.'

Pelham remembered the mum bank tellers of Britain.

'You worked in a bank?'

'That's right.'

'Do they all talk like you? In banks, I mean? In Australia?'

'Yeah. Why?'

'Are you going back to banking? When the war's over?'

'Nah. Gunna be a barrister.'

Still, almost nightly, he had the white manna of Moja's body. Only the heaviest cargoes of wounded, docking in Grevisa, kept them from each other. It seemed to him that as much as he needed the hot relief of penetrating Moja, he needed more the slow, all-night warmth of her back against his belly.

Her body amazed him with its quality. He began to think, women of forty are full women, women of twenty-three merely ripening.

At first, when he'd been less in love with her, he explored her body hesitantly. Like any young man with a measure of sexual arrogance, he feared coming across something, some flabbiness, some distortion of the limbs that would remind him they were, more or less, of different generations.

She was more perfect than he deserved and her perfection

was mysterious to him, oriental. Convinced of it herself, she could speak of her beauty without any embarrassment.

'The neat breasts,' she would say, 'are an indication of court fashion practically up into modern times. Trim ankles too, were everything. Similarly, lustrous hair. An interesting pubis. My father had an obsession about neat posteriors. And so I have my mother's sweet buttocks. A belly that swells gently but obviously from below the navel is also requisite in the Slavic world, as it was throughout Europe up to the Renaissance. Flat stomachs are a symptom of societies who have forgotten that woman is a symbol of the round earth. The society of Britain, for example. The society of the United States.'

She was, of course, a sexual education. When she moved her mouth between his thighs he found himself straining away from her, his hand stretched in front of him a little protectively. He had been taught only prostitutes did such things.

'Lovers have always done it,' she said. She was a little hurt.

He couldn't answer. A book a priest had lent him when he was seventeen said that some acts were unnatural. He didn't really believe it now. He was angry with himself. 'It's my upbringing,' he said.

There was an edge of genuine anger in Moja's voice. 'Don't use that as an excuse.'

Her hand played over his genitals like a bird preparing to nest.

'The big surgeon! The English are remarkable,' she told him. And she leaned towards him and bit his hip. 'Don't they teach their children *any* useful things?'

Magda knew about them. She would make a slight spitting noise whenever Moja passed. Pelham she considered an unjustly corrupted boy and lit candles for him. As if it would cure him of lechery, she saved for him the best dollops of goulash, the best cuts of *ražnici*.

Somehow, Moja and Pelham could tell that they were absolutely safe with Magda. Her contempt for Moja was of a more ancient brand, it was personal, it could not be resolved by appealing to commissars, who were a recent invention. Her concern for Pelham was ancient too, and maternal.

Binko, the blood-sucker, Magda's Serbian husband, would sometimes wink marginally at David; at other times give Moja's bottom a celebratory squeeze. He seemed to be saying, I am glad someone is loving and getting away with it.

The night of the crisis over Callaghan, David sat at table being solicitously overfed by Magda. Fielding was eating silently on one side of him. On the other, Cleary nagged him to be allowed to go on one of Southey's commando raids. The Irishman was losing his taste for independence. 'And I haven't had to guard your body once,' he kept telling David.

Moja entered, late for the meal. Magda hissed, cat, squaw, mother-judge. Moja was frowning and had no time for *that* game today.

'They have Callaghan. The commissars. He is being tried this moment.'

'What did he do?'

She looked at Pelham and spoke softly.

'He was found copulating, of course. With a partisan lady.'

Fielding said lazily, 'He'll talk his way out.'

Moja spoke in a tight knowing voice. 'They do not intend that he will. They intend execution to follow the trial. They will hand his body over to Southey. A warning, you see.'

They all got up and left the table. Magda came in groaning. She pleaded with them not to leave her meal. She thought it was all part of hussy Javich's malice.

Lawrence was drunk. So they took his truck without asking.

On the plateau, half a mile from the commissar's camp, partisan sentries stopped the truck. They argued with Moja. They were not awed, but neither was Moja. They told her no one British could be permitted to come any closer to the headquarters of the military commissar. But they could let her go on, alone.

'What can they do?' said Moja. 'They know I'm a friend of Tito's.'

'Don't go,' Pelham told her. He kneaded her arm, trying to detain her.

'Don't be neurotic, David.'

She put her hand on his a second. Little was gained, since both hands were numb with cold. She pulled away. Pelham and the others could hear her army boots crunching on the road towards the commissar's. It was a thin and ineffectual noise in the cold night.

The truck was backed. They drove to Southey's camp. The brigadier was combing his hair, ready for an evening at Moja's. The ends of his sandy moustache glistened.

'Nothing can be done,' he said. 'The bastard was warned . . .'

Pelham made a gesture of the hand but could not find the words to go with it. He was trying to say, Callaghan is a special case. The danger hadn't been explained to Callaghan in Callaghan's own language.

As David muttered, Southey hit his mantlepiece with a bunched fist. 'I suppose he's an exception,' he said.

The brigadier debated aloud with himself how it should be done. At last he called out Greenway's troop. They were kitted and armed as for a raid. From the top of the steps outside his billet, Southey inspected them. 'There isn't one of them that's not more important than that bastard,' he growled at David.

They climbed into trucks.

'You bring your vehicle in the rear, please,' Southey roared. It was a roar of anger, it was not warranted by the noise of other engines.

'Listen,' David told him, standing close to his ear. 'I won't be treated as if I'm responsible . . .'

'But you are responsible. You needn't have come and told me.'

The convoy crossed the plateau at good speed. David felt light in the hands and feet. Perhaps I am going into combat, against Moja's people. He pulled out the service revolver. He had taken only erratic care of it since he arrived on Mus. Sometimes he had used it to loose off shots at the morning patrol plane from the mainland. He had not had it cleaned since he left Italy. Now he found that there was only one round left in the clip.

Between David and Fielding, Cleary worked the mechanism of his Sten gun. That sound was clean, fluid.

'I've got an extra duty for you, Cleary. Every morning I want you to make sure there's a full clip in my revolver. Also I would like you to clean and oil the thing, once a week. Say Mondays.'

Cleary assured him, the way you answer a friend who has asked a favour. 'It'll be no trouble, no trouble at all.'

Fielding braked because the truck in front had stopped. Over the idling motors, David could hear loud Slavic cursing. At the cabin window commandos appeared, hustling disarmed partisan sentries. They were put in the rear of the truck. The convoy travelled a little way further. Then Southey had the troop dismount and form up. They marched crisply towards the commissar's house. David, Fielding, Cleary strode behind them. Stragglers and a little tentative.

The houses on the plateau formed no proper village. They stood obliquely to one another. Almost accidentally, they made an enclosed square. By moonlight, Greenway's troop marched into the square.

Southey strolled at the rear of the column. David said to him, 'The partisans might take it as a declaration of war. If you march in like this.'

Southey snorted. 'If they did, I'd be finished with the bastards.'

One single upstairs door opened at the top of an exterior stairway. Moja came out and looked down at the ranks of commandos. She seemed dimly to see that David was also there, behind the bulk of the troop. Then she turned her back and went indoors again.

'Where's that bloody commissar!' Southey began yelling, and somebody's dog replied. The brigadier's rage increased. He slapped his shoulder, as if feeling for the bow and quiver which were not there tonight.

He called out again. 'Mrs Javich. Tell them we are going to enter the houses.'

There was no answer. He told Greenway to divide the men into sections. The voice of Greenway was sharp and militant.

Moja again came out the door on to the landing. This time she walked down the stairs. She walked very slowly, like a hostage. David wanted to call to her but didn't know if it was wise. Was she a hostage? Did some mad commissar at an upstairs window have his sights trained on her? Trying not to run, he moved through the commandos to reach her. 'Exemplary,' she was telling Southey. 'They are quite genuine, as Callaghan has found out.'

'It's fair enough,' Southey said. 'They have us by the short and curlies.'

'Are you in danger?' David asked Moja.

'No. But we have to watch an execution.'

The commissar would let Callaghan go but he must watch the execution of the girl. Then all the soldiers on the island would be convinced and understand partisan discipline better.

Southey sent Moja back inside to consent. Meanwhile, he circled his men. 'Every man will be silent,' he said. 'You have no permission to boo or catcall.'

When Moja returned the third time, she was followed by a

squad of partisans. Next came Callaghan, hands roped, a heavy man at each elbow. Then a thin girl, similarly escorted. She sang a high mournful song at Callaghan's back. She had the same wide lost eyes you saw in all sensitive partisan women. Every second step or so she flinched as if expecting blows. There was no sign of them on her face however.

When Callaghan himself saw the troop there, formed up amongst the houses, he began yelling at them. He seemed to think that they too were parties to a conspiracy. That they would carry out the sentence. 'Pommy bastards!' he yelled. With the toes of his flying-boots he began to kick dirt in their direction. But his arms were so firm behind his back that he had no balance for it. While his guards pulled him up, he kept up the insults. 'I didn't have to fight for you bastards, you know. The British bloody Empire. I ought to be in the Pacific. Fighting Nips.'

It was clear. He thought he was making his death speech. Moja began shivering. David believed he could smell her tears, the salt of them. But here, at the centre of Mus, he could not touch her. Callaghan was led to Southey. The brigadier ordered commandos to close in about the boy. 'What is happening?' Callaghan asked. 'What's happening?'

The girl was put against the wall of the commissar's house. She crossed herself crookedly and continued to sing, tending to turn side on towards the wall, treating it as a confidant. The firing squad stood shoulder to shoulder, rather cramped, no more than ten feet from her.

'Holy Jesus,' David said.

'It's none of your business, David,' said the brigadier.

Callaghan writhed in strong arms and shouted his outrage, but no one took any notice. 'Christ,' he screamed. 'I'm talking to foreigners.'

A partisan officer realigned the woman to the wall. It was done gently. The woman looked at the ground. She said '*Nov!*'

three times slowly, directing the negative at the earth of Mus.

The officer gave three quick and undramatic commands. Next, only the frightful jolting noise of automatic weapons firing. Impacts lifted the girl and dropped her very flat. Already she seemed part of the landscape, scarcely distinct from the earth.

Before the partisans had picked her up, Southey was lecturing his commandos. 'I want you to tell all your comrades,' he said. 'We are under orders to accept partisan law. I have no orders to save anyone who falls foul of it. In fact, quite the contrary. Flying Officer Callaghan has been let go as a special concession, not as the result of our pressure. With him comes this message from the military commissar. No other allied soldier will be given a similar chance.'

As the troop marched away with the cautionary message, Southey turned to Callaghan. The young man breathed noisily, his eyes kept opening and shutting. When opened, the eyeballs stuck out. 'After the war, they'll try people like you and that bloody commissar,' said Callaghan. 'After the war, there'll be courts for it.'

The brigadier hit the boy on both cheeks and in the diaphragm. Callaghan could neither see nor find breath.

Pelham said, 'I am watching, Southey.'

'As you wish, David!' the brigadier told him.

So they went to find the trucks. When Callaghan had his breath back, he shook his head, all the time being forced along by commandos on either side. 'Bastards,' he said. 'Bastards.' He accused everyone. The Yugoslavs. The British. All Europe for its strife.

Suza had been so silent they all took her for granted. One afternoon, at the end of the operating list, Moja – who had been talking to her and receiving no answers – turned and saw that she was very close. In her hand a scalpel still stained from a recent jaw resection. Fielding, who had been septic nurse throughout the operation, had left the theatre. There were only Suza, scout nurse, scalpel at hand, and Mrs Javich, former anaesthetist to the Queen of Bulgaria.

Moja did not need to be told: Suza was jealous of her.

They fought. Moja took a long oblique wound in the lower arm. She felt decision and all her strength run from her like water from a holed bucket. It was only then that she began yelling for David and Cleary.

Cleary arrived first. Moja, whose ears were ringing, all her limbs numb, saw him hesitate in the doorway. Within a day or two, his hesitation would be easier to understand. Moja wanted to roar at him to hurry, but had no breath for it.

Suza's lethal fist with the scalpel in it was again raised. It hung there a while, as if Suza had forgotten her purpose. Soon its own weight would bring it down on Moja.

Cleary, once he made up his mind to move, exerted cruel pressure on her arm and took the weapon from her. Then, far more gently, he sat her on the floor in a corner of the theatre. She waited placidly. She had nothing to say.

Pelham ordered her sedated and put to bed. As he sutured the wound he questioned Moja about Suza's action.

'Does it mean she knows?'

'She couldn't know. But she can see you are more attentive to me than to her.'

'The situation's impossible.'

'No. But the poor girl is unbalanced. She should be sedated and shipped to Italy.'

'For God's sake. To protect us?'

'To protect herself.'

For the next two days, while Suza slept deeply, Pelham would often see Cleary near her bed. His jaw was always thrust sharply to one side of his face, a sign he was taking hard thought.

David had a tall Dickensian counting desk in one of the storerooms. Here he wrote letters and made notes in a ledger of the operations he had performed.

And here Cleary visited him soon after the attack on Moja. The Irishman's face had no expression, was flat and withdrawn.

Cleary said, 'I was hoping to talk to you, Captain. That's when you have the time . . .'

David was amused for a second by Cleary's return to titles. 'I have the time now, Private Cleary.'

Cleary seemed happy at the echo of institutional security involved in the use of *captain* and *private*.

'Perhaps you'd like to close the door,' David suggested.

Cleary closed it.

'It's Suza. I mean . . . I've had something to do with her.'

David's immediate anger was sapped by the thought that he himself was having something to do with Mrs Javich.

'I understand.'

'It was so bloody easy, sir. She seemed to be interested in . . . in you, you see. She seemed to be willing, so to speak, sir. To work her way up through the members of the surgical team.'

'And you encouraged that?'

'Not many would touch her after that first time she was questioned. Then Mrs Javich warned me off for a time. Then, since the Callaghan business . . . well, that really put a scare in us. But by then it was too late, sir. It's a bun in the oven she has, sir. She's conceived, as they say.' His voice became small and thin. 'She seems to think I'm the father.'

'And are you?'

'Well I must admit I could be, sir. You see, you frightened that orderly off her. That sort of left me, so to speak.'

David showed his teeth. 'You knew that put me in jeopardy?'

Cleary put his head on his wrist and shivered. 'I didn't really believe they were genuine, sir. Holy Mother, who could doubt them after the Callaghan business, though? Sir, I have to ask you to do a dreadful thing.'

132

'Abort her, I suppose you mean.'

'Yes, that's the dreadful thing I have to ask you.' He frowned devoutly. 'It's against me religion, sir.'

'Sod you, Cleary. It's against mine too.'

'Yes, sir,' Cleary said.

'The operation I'd like to do, Cleary, is a castration.'

'The horse has already galloped, sir,' Cleary said, head hung.

'Just the same. I wouldn't like you to underestimate the pleasure it would give me.'

'I can understand that, sir. But I know you're not a vengeful man, so to speak. Will you do it, sir, and save two lives?'

Of course, Pelham thought, some doctors can. Better men than me. They were not raised to see the aborting of a foetus as murder.

David remembered an abortion he had witnessed once in a London hospital. It was medically necessary. But the four-month old foetus had not known that and had still visibly struggled and died hard at the hands of surgeons fifty times its weight.

'I'll tell you what I can do, Cleary. I can diagnose her for a disease she hasn't got and send her back to Bari by trawler. It has not escaped my notice that the Italians do not shoot women for bearing children.'

Cleary slapped his leg. 'Sir, how can I thank you?'

'Keep trace of Suza, that's how.'

When the *Rake's Progress* visited Mus, Suza was once more sedated. A card saying *Chronic rheumatic myocarditis* was tied to her wrist.

She had always been such a mute young woman, except for the day she damaged Moja. No one had special farewells for her, little mementoes to press in her hands. Pelham patted her blonde hair out of pity. She was driven away.

At dawn, however, she was brought back. With her came a note from Hugo Peake, port commander of Mus.

It read: 'Bad luck, old chap. The commissars got wind. They were pretty pissed off about that other lady you sent away to Italy with a tag on her wrist. I'm afraid they don't believe anything's wrong with this Suza lady. Don't try it any more, will you, David? We need the space for other things.'

In the past days, Cleary had entered the hospital in a jaunty, tread-on-the-tail-o'-me-coat manner. Seeing Suza that morning, tucked up again in a hospital cot, still sedated for the journey she would not make, he began to limp.

'All right,' he told David. He was not begging any more. He had dignity. 'I want to go on one of those commando raids. I won't be shot by those Marxist bastards.'

David believed he intended to go missing on Korčula or Hvar, to inhabit their olive forests, or live like a fox in the caves on the highest slopes of the hills. Maybe he deserved to have to do that, David decided. But even then David knew that in the end the abortion would be performed.

'You and she can communicate with each other?'

Cleary blushed. 'We can make ourselves understood.'

'Instruct her in the symptoms of appendicitis. Teach her to wince and groan when I palpate her abdomen. Do you understand? In a week or two, when the commissars are thinking of other things, I'll take her appendix out.'

'You shouldn't have to, sir,' said Cleary. It was a sort of apology.

'Get out of my sight,' said David.

It was not a hypocritical anger, he tried to tell himself. He was uncomfortable at having to change his principles so close to the German invasion date, so close to massacre and mass burial.

A week later, when the Jaegers had once again failed to arrive, David extracted Suza's appendix. While the abdomen was opened, he found the uterus. It had certainly begun to distend. He touched it with his gloved hand, but a feeling akin

134

to nausea swept him and the flesh behind his ears tightened. It was a sensation he had never felt when faced with any other organ. Perhaps he feared strong movement within the uterine sac, even though it was at this stage medically unlikely. At last he squeezed the uterus firmly. It was twenty seconds' work, no more. Soon after the operation the small corpse would pass, barely noticed, from her body.

His work on Suza seemed to emphasize the question of Moja. For the first time he began to think of it as the problem of Moja. Now that he knew they might survive he began to ask himself questions. Do I love Moja? Yes, there was no doubt. I remain sane in her twin climates – her genial sexuality by night, her control of the hospital by day.

He felt the discontent that anyone feels who is loving a colleague on the quiet, yet must perform clear, hard-headed work with her professionally. The way we have to carry ourselves in the daytime, Pelham thought, is unreal.

He was sure she could talk the commissars into letting her marry him, while he might be able to persuade Southey. He felt distaste however for the idea that age would mark her, years before it touched him. A Moja who aged before he did would still be Moja, he thought. Why am I frightened by the idea?

Of course, it was also a rule of his class. One was not supposed to marry the natives. One could get away with marrying a Frenchwoman or a German, or even a certain kind of Spaniard. To marry a Slav, and a Slav thirteen years your senior, disqualified you from the fashionable London medicine he had a mind to practise after the war. These were indecent and paltry considerations. But they counted for him. He could not help them counting.

He thought, if I were a better man I would marry Moja and live with her on one of these sublime islands, when they become sublime again. I'd practise a better medicine than Bersak's.

People like Jovan and Peko would surround us. We'd drink *prošek* together in the long evenings.

For some reason, the location of his hospital was still a military secret. Therefore he received no supplies from medical stores in Italy. He worked with supplies diverted from Bersak's hospital.

Pelham also found himself using quantities of Italian drugs and material. It seemed that in some areas the Italians had surrendered their hospitals directly to the partisans. Wherever the gauze and plaster, ether and sulpha came from, they were quickly used up. For, besides battle casualties, many asinine mishaps occurred on Mus.

There were, for example, the mines. The assaults from Mus against nearby islands had so stung the enemy that German sappers were mining the beaches of Hvar, Korčula, Lastovo. Partisan guerrilas would watch from the forests. At night they would come down to the beaches and dig up the mines. To avoid disturbing the garrison's sense of security, they always smoothed the beach over again.

The fused mines would then be loaded on trawlers and brought to Mus. Donkey carts hauled them up on to the plateau from the ports of Grevisa and Mus. On the plateau, they were buried. In this way the commissars prepared minefields of their own against an invasion. The mine planting was haphazard, however, and no markers were placed.

Refugees billeted on the plateau, children, partisans, commandos, began to be brought into Pelham's hospital with limbs blown off them. Southey said that at least twice a day he heard the thump of a mine exploding under someone's foot.

On a day when Lawrence was bringing stolen supplies of plaster from Mus to Grevisa, a fat bomber crept over the slope of Mushtar and set its nose for his truck. He braked and ran across open ground to a slight hollow. He dropped there and waited, not looking. He heard large thuds all around him but no explosions. He looked up and saw the air was full of white dust. It landed thickly on his lips and soon it formed a paste. The enemy was bombing his truck with bags of flour, using him to train a bombardier.

He felt enraged, more than he would have if the missiles had had warheads. The fliers above him were the same sort of smart flippant aviator as had, in a different uniform and different language, seduced his West Country wife. 'Fight fair,' he screamed at them. It was as if he were begging them to use tracer and high explosive.

As he stood cursing them, they turned for another run. He saw a fat flour bag leave the undercarriage and turn end over end, a lazy, angled descent. He was sure it would take him in the chest, yet he did not move. Ten points for the trainee bombardier, he thought ironically.

In fact it flew over his right shoulder. Yet its impact with the earth lifted him, made an attempt to pull his legs from his trunk, landed him forehead first against the tailboard of his truck. That contemptuous flour bag had struck a mine.

The bomber banked homeward. Bleeding from the hairline, blood vivid against his whitened face and uniform, he drove down to Grevisa. He was slower and less sure on the hillside than ever he was when drunk.

'Bloody airmen,' he muttered all the time. 'Bloody glamour boys.'

He parked his truck and staggered to the hospital. Suza, standing in the sunlight, saw him first, all white and vivid red. She grew hysterical. At the noise, Cleary came out to help him.

'You look like a pillar of salt, man,' Cleary told him. Lawrence tried to hit the Irishman.

From that day forward Sergeant Lawrence was finished.

He never drove again, but limped around Grevisa frowning and rarely talking. Sometimes he would wander into the wards and stand by the beds of the drugged, the delirious. In a dull voice he would tell them: 'Rip your stitches out. We're all going to die.'

There was no trawler to take him back to Italy. Pelham tried to keep him out of the hospital but could spare no one to watch him all the time. At last David discussed it with Lawrence's deputy, a young corporal called Mayhew.

'You'll have to make sure he takes his sedatives.'

'Maybe we ought to let him wander about, sir. He's been through a lot.'

'I know. But he can't be allowed to frighten the wounded.'

Yet Mayhew seemed to think Lawrence had earned the right to behave madly. The two of them had been together in the desert. They had travelled deep into an enemy hinterland with raiding parties of the Long Range Desert Force. In little hard-held pockets of earth they had treated terrible wounds. On the run they had shut off spurting haemorrhages.

Now Mayhew worked as if he were saying, Sergeant Lawrence may be off-balance now, but when he was on, this was the sort of professional he made of me.

Mayhew was especially good at sorting wounded.

Before the *Rake's Progress* sailed back to Italy, a Liberator came down into the sea near Mus. Both its survivors were brought into the hospital. One had a crushed leg. Some equipment in the cockpit had flown loose and done the injury.

This patient was New England genteel. A little over twenty, blue-eyed, responsible-looking. It seemed that someone had helped him, crushed leg and all, out of the plane and into the slipstream. This someone had then jumped himself but drowned after entering the sea. The boy was aware of it. In a quiet, almost scholarly way, he raved about the concepts of plan and chance. Like a philosophy major, he was able to quote Kant, Spinoza, Hegel.

David cut the leg off. For too many days afterwards, the boy showed symptoms of shock. His blood pressure stayed low, his pulse was rapid and thin. His eyes were wide. He seemed indifferent to the pain in his stump or in the phantom leg. It seemed he had other problems.

'Is anything the matter?' David asked him.

'You didn't tell me the whole story,' the boy said. He had a wry smile. He looked as if he were trying to show he knew how to appreciate some black cosmic joke. But he was too boyish to bring it off.

'The whole story?'

'I thought in the services they treated you to the truth. That boozy sergeant of yours, it took him to let me have it.'

'Have what? I don't understand.'

'He sat down by me and told me I had blood poisoning. I could tell he was telling the truth because he leant over me and started howling.'

'When was this?'

'The night of the operation.'

David thought, I'll go and shake Lawrence. Then he remembered it was no use shaking psychiatric cases. Shell shock, wife-loss, booze – whatever the cause, poor Lawrence should not be shaken.

'Listen to me. You've lost a leg. But you're going to live.'

'He cried over me.' The boy still believed tears to be the final criterion.

'He's a lunatic, that's why. Now I want your blood pressure up, and your pulse slow and stronger. I want you to concentrate on the pain in your stump. That's better than believing the sergeant.'

He moved away. The boy called after him.

'Then he shouldn't be round here. He's a public danger.'

When Pelham went hunting for Lawrence, he found him standing in the street, in the thin winter sun. He was just like one of those psychiatric cases who stands riveted to a spot on the earth, because to choose a particular direction is far too difficult. Pelham spoke gently to him. He reminded him of the lie that had struck at the pulse rate of the young American.

'Why did you do it?' he asked Lawrence.

Lawrence looked absently out across the harbour of Grevisa. The blue spine of Korčula looked glacial today. He squinted and gestured a little with his hand. Pelham noticed the big farm callouses on it.

'Those airforce chaps. They seem to have everything tied up. The war. Women . . . I didn't think it would do any harm. Not to an airforce chap.'

When Lawrence went aboard the *Rake's Progress* to leave Mus, he was not conscious. He had been given laudanum in his coffee.

One night they lay naked under a blanket, listening to the *bora* roar down on Mus from the north. He thought he wanted to lie like this forever with Moja, within sound of the *bora*, their sweat running together from the high effort of erotic climax.

'Moja, I think we ought to be married,' he murmured, surprising himself.

As soon as he said it, he realized it had not come out very felicitously. He heard her laugh deeply at his side, he felt her rib-cage vibrate against his with laughter. But this kind of laughter was not welcome. It was the sort of affectionate sound mothers make when a child brings home some inappropriate gift.

She imitated a Belgravia drawl. 'They'd all say, old Pelham, he married one of the wogs, didn't you hear?'

'It's what Pelham loves,' he muttered. 'Damn what they'd say.'

'It could end your career. After the war.'

In the absence of an invasion, it seemed more and more likely he would have such a career.

'You would hate me for killing your chances,' she said.

'If I were married to you I would simply have to rise above pettiness.'

Suddenly Moja was up, stamping up and down, naked on the bare boards. 'Christ,' she said. 'Christ!' It was hard to believe in her anger with her breasts and nipples quivering, distracting him. For emphasis, she picked up a carafe that stood on a chest of drawers and shattered it against the woodwork. Distantly, Pelham could hear Binko and Magda discussing the sudden noise.

'Christ, now you've spoilt everything, David. What do you think Moja Javich is? Some sort of moral gymnasium? You go to it to build your moral muscle? To learn to rise above *pettiness*? Jesus! No man has ever insulted me so much.'

David was sitting up, very cold. But he did not get under the blankets in case that proved him callous. 'I wasn't aware . . .'

She stood still, her succulent legs apart, her pubis thrust forward, her fist raised towards the ceiling. 'Don't you know there are only three good reasons for marrying a woman? One is if she has a title, two is if she's rich, three is if the centre of the world is between her thighs.'

'That's a very continental outlook.'

'You British always say *continental* as if you're talking about a race of cannibals.'

'The third of the reasons applies in this case anyhow.'

'Oh yes! I noticed that by the way you spoke. You talked about what *ought* to be done. Why didn't you speak in terms of the blood in your groin?'

'You know. The British aren't a demonstrative race.'

'Christ.'

'Sometimes it seems . . . I'm just making use of you.'

'Have you asked yourself? Perhaps women like usage?'

'Do you mean you don't *want* to marry me?'

Without answering she grabbed her boots and army trousers, her shirt, her jacket, her frayed underwear. She walked out, her neat backside tensed in anger.

He had two nights to consider the insult he had paid her. The first thing she said when she began talking to him again, was, 'I was so disappointed in you, that was all.'

Within a week, they were sleeping together again. The sexual cringes appropriate to his upbringing kept recurring. I am using her, he sometimes told himself, as if she were a whore or a girl at a hunt ball.

Chapter 8 X-Ray

On the one day two mines were detonated on the plateau. One blew the leg off a commando. The other destroyed the goat of a seven-year-old boy refugee. The child himself took nine fragments in the stomach. Looking at the child, Pelham said, 'Wouldn't you think they'd send me a bloody X-ray machine?'

'I'll get you an X-ray machine,' said Moja.

'How? Requisition one off Magda?'

'I said I'd get you an X-ray machine.'

'How?'

'*How* will look after itself. *When* is a small problem. It might take as long as a month.'

The child was anaesthetized. Fielding swabbed his wounds with spirit. When David began cutting, he found that two of the wounds were minor. The liver, however, had a ragged wound. The extraction of the steel, the suturing of the organ went well. He began to smile to himself.

'You don't believe you're getting the X-ray machine,' Moja accused him.

'Perhaps not.'

'You'll see.'

When he emerged from the theatre, Cleary was waiting for him.

'There's flyers in the mess, sir.'

143

'Flyers?'

'American. They landed on the new strip. Bringing cargo to the engineers.'

Moja stood nearby, tapping the saline drip of the unfortunate goat boy.

'Moja,' said Pelham. 'Come with me?'

She hesitated, not wanting to leave the child in this postoperative state.

'We have to speak to some pilots.' he said. 'Charm may be needed.'

The three airmen they found in the mess were badly dressed in leather jackets and battered headgear. They hung around the piano and one of them was playing Gershwin poorly. When Pelham and Moja entered, one of them called out, 'Welcome.'

They had flown in in a Dakota.

'What did you carry?' Pelham asked them.

'Cement mixers, gravel. Beer.'

'Are you going back empty?'

'Nothing to take.'

'Oh, Jesus.' Pelham put his hand over his eyes a second at the thought of unused cargo space.

'We have wounded,' Moja told them. 'When we can, we send them back by trawler. It isn't good for people with belly or thoracic wounds.'

'You want us to fly them out?'

'In a word,' said Pelham.

'We can't do anything for them while we're in flight,' said an infant sergeant who must have been cargo-master. 'If they started a bleed or something. Or bust their stitches . . .'

His pilot, the piano-player, waved him silent. 'Wait. What about that crazy Belinda?'

The co-pilot said, 'And her friend . . . er . . . Denise.'

The pilot composed his face to make a promise. 'Listen, next time we come – four days, give or take the weather –

we'll bring army nurses.'

It was so fantastic a promise Pelham did not believe it. But four days later he had a telephone call from the airstrip. 'Doctor, the Dakota's in. Can you get your wounded up here?'

An hour later David arrived by truck at the clay scar on the plateau where, somehow, his Dakota pilot had landed safely twice over. On the edge of the field, the cargo-master sat on a small heap of supplies and watched two US Army nurses taking snapshots of Yugoslavs and the mountain.

'Can I load the wounded?' Pelham asked.

'Yeah. And these are yours.' The cargo-master tapped the cartons he sat on.

'These?'

'I've got a list. There's Vitamins. Coagulants, Vitamin K. Anti-coagulants. Narcotics. Antihistamines. Penicillin.'

'Do I have to sign?'

'It ain't that sort of supplies.'

'Isn't it?' Pelham laughed and the cargo-master laughed slyly with him. 'Where's your pilot?'

In fact the pilot had arrived and was peering up at the port engine of his plane. 'Hope it's to your satisfaction,' he muttered over his shoulder.

Pelham came close to him, secretively.

'Can you get me an X-ray machine?'

'An X-ray machine? Jesus!'

'Not that I'm not grateful for this . . .'

'I'll ask our source.'

A week later the Dakota landed once more but although it brought more drugs, the pilot said the source had laughed at the idea of an X-ray machine. There hadn't been any call for one, said the source, until now.

Pelham knew what the source meant: there had been no call for one on the black market. The drugs that now came in each week were a siphoning-off from that same market, a sop, a donation. Pelham did not complain. He had a sailor with a lump out of his chest and a burgeoning pelvic ulcer. He could feed the man penicillin and fly him away from Mus. Neither he nor the man cared under whose auspices it would all happen.

The runway was still not long enough to be safe for bombers and fast fighters. The ancient vines of Mus grew well down into the plain. They were the oldest vines in Europe, the phylloxera epidemic of 1866 had not reached them. The commissars fought against any yardage the Texan major and his engineers wanted to take at the expense of the vines. So the airfield was still incomplete when an American Lightning fighter, engine stuttering, roared in over Grevisa. On the plateau the Americans agreed to talk him down. It would be harder for him than for Callaghan. A Lightning, even though misfiring, needed more room.

On landing, the pilot braked madly. Deep tyre marks were burned into the earth. He finished with reeking wheels, tail up, nose down, on the edge of the vines.

He was Polynesian, probably Hawaiian. A reconnaissance pilot. He'd been over Austria, taking photographs. 'They're hot snaps,' he assured everyone. 'Just fix the engine, willya?'

The mechanics told him his engine would need a lot of fixing. At least six hours.

'There's seven hundred guys waiting for these pix,' he protested at the top of his voice. 'Just fix it enough for from here to Italy. I can spare two hours.'

For the two hours, the pilot stood behind the mechanics and nagged them. They got his port engine to go, but raggedly. He alone smiled at the noise.

Commandos, American engineers, even the partisans spent the time uprooting vines. Which had been spared a European epidemic only to fall to the insistence of an Hawaiian pilot.

'Time up,' he said, raising his hand. The Texas major said, 'Someone tell those frigging partisans not to stand across the end of the runway.'

For the partisans always watched take-offs head on, as if no other angle of observation would suit them.

Someone neglected to carry out the major's order, or was unable to.

The pilot roared his engine and rolled down the strip without having had any sign of consent from the major. Very soon he got into the air and was climbing steeply, one wing higher than the other. 'Too steep, too steep,' the major yelled.

At the peak of its climb, the plane fell silent. It turned on its lower wing and fell amongst the partisans. From Mus to Grevisa the explosion was heard, and then reheard as an echo from the sides of Mushtar.

The noise, the intense flowering of yellow flame, snatched away the breath of all witnesses, the major's as well. It was ten seconds before that officer had breath for an order. While his jeep raced to the crash, there was a second explosion. Gobs of blazing fuel landed amongst the injured and on the earth of the airstrip. There were eight partisan dead. Seven more died of burns before they got to Grevisa. Eight or nine others crawled around, beating at the flames, their heads aflame, their backs, their arms.

The worst case was the pilot. He had lurched from the wreckage. One of the engineers put out his fires by rolling him in a blanket. His face and fingers had been burnt off. His hands became a weepy, red mess. 'I'm the pilot,' he told the men who handled him.

He was taken to Pelham's hospital with the others. When David examined him, he thought, this is the worst case I've ever seen. He began to sweat.

Christ, he thought, I don't want to touch this man. He looked at the patches of flying helmet and fibres of uniform that had been burnt into the seeping skin.

'Why can't I see anything?' the Polynesian asked.

Without thinking about it, David lied. 'We'll have you seeing,' he said, in the jovial tones GPs use in cottage hospitals.

'Hey, you a doctor?'

'Yes. We're going to give you an anaesthetic and fix up your face.'

'You gonna photograph me?'

'Why would we photograph you?'

'So I can see what I was like. When I've got better.' All this was said in a whistling voice and with hard breathing. I shouldn't be talking to him, Pelham admitted.

'I can't help you, I'm afraid. No cameras.'

They got him to the table. Moja tried to put the pentothal in but couldn't find a vein. 'Hurry, hurry, Mrs Javich,' David told her, reverting to formal titles in this high crisis.

He felt calmer when the pentothal was in and the plasma flowed. He began working on the face with sterile saline, swabbing delicately. Suddenly the man threatened to choke. It was oedema, the bloating of the windpipe. Fielding had the scalpel to hand. David cut a hole in the trachea, just under the Adam's apple. They had no proper equipment for tracheotomy, but Fielding supplied a length of rubber tubing from the plasma kit. Next Pelham ran a long and similar piece of tubing through the man's mouth down into the stomach. One had to presume the man would want and need meals.

'Could you respirate him?' Pelham asked Fielding.

Fielding, translator of the *Kosovo*, obeyed. David finished the cleaning. He dusted the face and arms with penicillin, but could spare only sulpha for the rest of the body. He wrapped the man in padding to absorb the exudate.

Then he encased the head in plaster. Only the breathing and feeding tubes and the left ear were exempt. By the small hours of the next morning, the Hawaiian was conscious. He lay in his plaster helmet, unable to speak or swallow. Yet when the plaster was tapped he made tiny movements with his hands. Jovan got instructions on how to feed him. Thin soup was to be poured down the stomach pipe by means of a funnel. Jovan was warned that if the soup went into the breathing pipe, the Hawaiian would drown.

For two days Magda sat by the Hawaiian and crooned Serbo-Croat tendernesses into his exposed ear. He replied sometimes with small grunts and hand movements. He was making with Magda a language appropriate to his condition. Then, just as Jovan arrived with a cup of thin soup, she was aware that the normal hissing from the lower of the two tubes had stopped. He had died his blind, enclosed death.

Moja brought the news to him in his small office-storeroom. He nodded and knew he should not be surprised. He took her small hands and saw how the knuckles were vellum-smooth and blue-white from all the scrubbing-up she did for surgery. He raised the hands to his mouth.

'Skin,' he said. 'Skin.'

'He would have been comatose,' she told him, implying a painless death.

Pelham said sentimentally, 'I hope he was dreaming of Hawaii.'

That night David ate alone, though not by design. It was just that Fielding, Cleary, even Moja, had eaten earlier. Magda did not complain of his tardiness. She enjoyed having him to herself. She fussed around him, topping his glass whenever he took a sip. She had few doubts that wholesome food would improve his morals.

Moja came in and assessed Magda's motherly behaviour with cold eyes. 'Get out!' she said.

Magda planted her feet and faced her old enemy. But Moja

had no time for the normal swapping of abuse. She picked up a vase of winter violets from the table and hurled them at the hearth 'Get out!' she repeated.

Since the cook was not hurt and was even grateful to be reinforced in her ideas about Madame Javich, Pelham began to smile, covering himself with his hand. He was tickled by Moja's strange, unsocialist, aristocratic antipathy to Magda.

Magda went slowly. The sway of her large hips said, I'm glad to be out if you're going to use such low methods.

'David,' said Moja.

'We seem to have all our important conversations in here,' David remarked. But he was a little frightened. Her blue eyes were blank, as if she were just any vacant, pretty woman.

'I'm going.'

'What do you mean?' He felt his stomach cramping.

'They have dropped a Canadian doctor into Bosnia. He has asked that I come and set up his house.'

He stood up. He felt panic at first and crazily looked at the door as if he needed a line of flight. Next he thought, without her there's nothing but weariness, the long surgical lists and no comfort at the end of them.

'Set up his house?' he asked. He couldn't believe it.

'Yes.'

'Sod his house.'

She put a hand up to his face, to calm him.

'You're *willing* to go. You actually think it's a good thing.'

'Who can say?' She smiled at him. He threw out his arms and clamped her against him.

'Arrange it, please, Moja.'

'You know I can't, my love.'

'What will I do?'

'You'll be all right. You know you're fragile. That's your strength, David. Your humility saves you, my love. Now listen.' She stroked the line of his jaw. 'Our little love. It seems wide as the world to us. But it doesn't count. The tides of history count.'

'I don't believe that.'

'No. Maybe I don't either. But they believe it very hard and strong in Jajce. So don't argue, eh? My trawler for the mainland has already berthed in Mus. My replacement is being briefed at commissar headquarters.'

Pelham wanted to know what sort of bloody replacement. It was up to him to approve a replacement, as much as it was any damn commissar's business.

'She's nothing sinister. She's a girl. Very quiet, very competent. Her name is Jela.'

If Moja had said aloud, she'll be better for you than I am, David would have been tempted to hit her. Yet the assertion hung in the air.

They stood together. They began weeping. They pulled at each other's bodies as if there was some nourishment at the core which they needed.

'You have been such a clever boy,' she told him. 'You are a worthy doctor and a clever boy.'

There was no time for parties and farewells in the mess. They would have been intolerable in any case.

Mayhew, Lawrence's successor, drove them down to Mus. She shivered in the cold air of the plateau. 'I hate sea journeys,' she said. 'A silly thing. Hydrophobia. However, it won't take long.'

It was a bright night. In spite of the cold, the moonlight threw an exotic, North African radiance over the whitewashed town. Hugo Peake was there to say goodbye, and the ancient admiral, Sir Martin Harris.

Looking up, David found that he could see, sharply enough, the rigging of her ship against the bright moon. Hugo Peake got a lantern from his office and forced it on the captain of the trawler. 'So you can signal more easily if my chaps challenge you. Mind you, I want it back.'

The trawler captain accepted the lamp with some contempt and sent one of his crew down into the hold with it. Peake saw David had noticed the slapdash disappearance of the lamp. 'They'll be right,' he said. 'The enemy patrols have just about given up the night to us.'

When it was time, David went aboard with her. 'Don't go,' he kept hissing at her.

'Be kind to me,' she said. 'Make it less difficult, David.'

But when the trawler cast off, Pelham hugged her in open grief and desire. He had to jump the small leeway the boat had made. On the dock, amongst his po-faced fellow countrymen, he wept without stint. They put half-embarrassed hands on his shoulders and fed him more of the slivovitz.

Next morning, very early, a milk-white girl stepped inside the hospital door. Mayhew's orderlies noticed her. Her white neck rose so sweetly out of the coarse army shirt she wore.

Pelham was fetched. When he walked into the wards he saw the girl leaning over the bed of a refugee woman and weeping softly. Exquisite weeping from a lean, soft girl. He resented her unreasonably and on sight for her apparent lack of a hard core and for turning up in Moja's empty place.

'You are the new girl?'

'Jela, captain doctor.'

'Don't cry, Jela.' He only half-managed to make an order.

'It is all right,' she said, continuing to cry. 'Pulmonary tuberculosis,' she stated, nodding at the woman in the bed.

'That's right.'

'And she is with a child, captain doctor?'

'Yes. She's pregnant.' In fact, you could just see the pregnancy beneath the blanket. Some scrawny foetus dwelt in there, a sailor in a diseased ship. Through the mother's nose ran a firm rubber tube, draining the mess out of her trachea. She got daily, wasteful injections of appropriate drugs. They came too late for her. This winter there had been too much night marching for her, too much cold sleeping in barns. The birth of her child would certainly stop her heart, but he did not tell that to the exquisite soft weeper.

'When is she due?'

'Very soon by *her* calculations. If she's correct.'

The girl started cleaning her tears up with a big manly grey handkerchief, acquired from somebody's army.

'You must,' she said, 'find a woman in milk to feed the baby.'

'Yes, yes.'

They heard the breath grate in and out of the woman's mouth. David wanted to get away from that bed. Every time he saw this patient, he wanted to kill her with an overdose. Then other cases would distract him and he would not think of the question of the tubercular woman for another day. If you gave her her peace with morphine, you could then extract the baby from the dead womb. Yet it would not live. It would need to be put in the sophisticated cubicles you find only in large city hospitals. Its best chance on Mus was for it to be born when it felt ready and robust enough.

David thought, if this girl will only move away from the bed, I can forget the question till tomorrow.

'I'll show you the theatre,' he said. 'You are a nurse?'

'I am trained in Slovenia,' she said, as energetically as if it were a political slogan.

'Slovenia,' she said again, quietly enough, but in the manner of someone naming her favourite football team.

'Oh?' He saw no particular significance in Slovenia.

'Ljubliana Hospital.' That was meant to drive the point home.

'I see. Is Ljubliana Hospital good?'

She whispered, in case anyone's professional pride was hurt. 'Ljubliana medicine is the only good medicine in the whole of the country. It is Vienna medicine. It is not farm medicine. The Croatians, the Bosnians, the Serbs – all horse-butchers!'

'Mrs Javich never mentioned it.'

There was a mild quiver of ancient prejudice in the milk-white girl. 'Mrs Javich is a Serb. And a grand lady.'

'So she is.' To David, her summary of Moja sounded like something she had picked up overnight from the commissars, something to give her the impetus to out-Javich Javich. It would never be done.

He called for Sergeant Fielding to show the girl the theatre drill of the place. 'Find out if she knows her business,' he whispered to Fielding.

He had already forgotten about the tubercular woman-with-child.

The woman Jela had wept over went into labour earlier than Pelham had expected. It was a terrible birth. Pelham could not deliver the child by caesarian section because the pentothal would kill the woman. It would then take some fast butchery to drag out her child before it asphyxiated. The woman had no breath left for the act of childbirth. She lay heaving and purple, her screams were a weird whistle from her collapsing lungs. She needed cylinders of oxygen and carbon dioxide if she were to have the luxury of a full-scale scream.

At her head stood Jela with a pad of ether. It was against the rules to etherize a patient with respiratory failure. But the woman deserved a little mercy. So at the corner of her agony stood Jela with a pad. Jela, of course, wept throughout.

The little head appeared. A large cranium. The right shoulder, the right arm. Pelham would by now willingly have chosen the caesarian method to save the woman her pain. It was too late. 'Not long,' he promised.

The child proved to be a boy.

When Pelham held the baby up and set its breathing going

with a slap on the rump, he hoped – maybe sentimentally – that the woman could see her son. She gave no sign. He noticed the skin of her face was purple, her fingernails too.

Fielding snipped the umbilicus and Peko, the Yugoslav orderly, wrapped the boy in a towel.

'Give it to Jela,' Pelham ordered. It was done.

Jela went off to wash the child. The noises it made were not those of a strong child. There were little creaks of protest that passed for crying.

Meanwhile the woman made the terrible panicking noises of pulmonary collapse. 'Fielding,' David whispered. 'Fill a syringe with morphine. Keep her under till her heart fails.'

'It should have been done a week ago, sir.'

'You're probably right.'

'The child won't live anyhow. A skinned rabbit.'

'Well, do it now.'

David waited by the woman, holding her by the pulse. 'Soon,' he whispered at her. 'Soon.'

On a Tuesday late in March, bombers came twice to the island, bombing both ports and the plateau, and twice again on the Wednesday. There were few casualties. The partisans kept only a small force in the ports by day, reinforcing them at night, while the plateau was thick with shelters and anti-aircraft guns. But the raids depressed people and showed that the enemy's High Command still had the intention to invade.

Between raids, Jela interviewed the scrawny refugee women on the plateau, seeking a wet-nurse for the new child. The infant's stomach rejected diluted cow's milk or glucose and water and its life hung on her faint chance of finding a buxom nursing woman in the refugee camp. She discovered one. A robust girl still suckling her own boy, who was two and a half years old. Jela bullied the woman back to the hospital and fed her heartily. There was enough milk for both the boy of two years and the boy of two days.

Pelham saw that being a foster mother had made Jela more resilient. He did not feel resilient himself. In the solitary bedroom to which his rank and status entitled him, he would wake up muttering protests. 'No, no,' he'd find himself saying, thinking that the Jaegers already had him in their hands.

He slept better when the commissars suddenly ordered him to transfer his hospital to the plateau. He believed the plateau might hold for a long time. Now that it had an airstrip, he might even be ordered to fly out with the wounded. On the plateau he would be as lonely, reaching out for Moja and finding only the non-plastic air. But he was a better life risk.

Busy at the hospital, David let Mayhew and Fielding look for the new hospital site. They took Cleary along, for his native wit.

At the south-west end of the inland plain they found a little hamlet, some barns, five two-storey houses. All of them had good cellars, apparently untouched: the commissars did not permit looting. Only one of the five houses was occupied. An old woman was ailing, all by herself in a brass bed, under a canopy of vivid scarlet and yellow needlework. Fielding saw Cleary bend over the woman, saying, 'You look like a good place to be starting a hospital, little mother.'

To these five houses in the unexpected village of Momoulje, the equipment, the staff, the patients were removed over a period of days. The Georgian hospital of Gievisa had finished its second spate as a battle surgery.

In the first days of April, Cleary installed his generator in a storeroom at the back of the house which was Theatre and Intensive Care Ward. The lights came on over the operating table.

Pelham looked with apathy on these small miracles. He approached the worst wounds with the same apathy. There were, he felt, hundreds of flabbergasting wounds behind him and hundreds still to face.

Good Friday restored him. That day a squad of dusty partisans, driving pack asses, arrived in front of the hospital at Momoulje. The officer began yelling for Dr Pelham.

David had been sleeping. He came downstairs, drowsy and anxious. When he walked into the open the partisan officer smiled and made a gesture of the hand that said *all the cargo is yours*. Partisans began unloading paper parcels, brought them into the mess, dropped them on the floor.

'What is it?' David asked the officer. All the officer would say was *Moja Javich*.

He picked up one of the parcels and weighed it in his hands. He tore the cord. It cut his index finger. Under the paper was a shiny metal armature. Fielding, Cleary, Jela had come downstairs and were also unwrapping. They too held up pieces of some puzzling mechanism. They dropped them and opened some more. At last, Fielding understood.

'Do you know what this is? This is an X-ray machine.'

The partisan officer slapped his hip affirmatively. 'Moja Javich,' he told them again.

Jela translated the man's story, perhaps a little reproachfully. You could just see, looking hard, that she didn't like speaking out the triumph of another woman. Before leaving Mus (she translated), Moja arranged a raid. *This* raid. One of the partisans on the island had worked in the dispensary of a general hospital in Split. It had an excellent radiology department. The raiders travelled from Mus to Split by fishing boat. Like bona fide fishermen, they came ashore close to the wall of Diocletian's palace and entered the city by one of its ancient gates. They walked a kilometre to the general hospital. Their arms were hidden under their fishermen's coats or in sacks over their backs. They infiltrated the kitchens and the Outpatients' Department. Casually, they held up the Radiology Section. Only a sleepy radiologist and a young Croatian resident were on duty. The X-ray machine was German, and the partisans unbolted it piece by piece, having been told by Moja to do the work gently. They were more than an hour at the task. As each part was dismantled, they wrapped it in brown paper and tied it with string. The paper and string were supplied by the young Croatian doctor. It was clear he begrudged them the commodities. His sympathies were not partisan.

As the parcels were wrapped, partisans loaded them into sacks and departed. There was a bay south of Split where the raiders were to wait for a trawler.

The last of the partisans did not leave Split with the last of the mechanism until dawn had broken. The streets were full of Yugoslavs going to work and German soldiers marching off on various details.

Pelham put his arm around the partisan officer. Dried sweat, bad teeth, much celebratory rakia gave the man a strange animal smell which David was willing to savour.

'You should be given a medal,' he told the partisan. 'A medal, tovarich.'

They removed all the parts to a small room behind the operating theatre. There they worked all afternoon, engrossed, trying to fit one piece of metal to another. Laughing, cursing jovially. They had sent for the American engineers and for the commando electricians. Pelham secretly doubted whether anyone could do much with the jumble of parts. For the moment he was content to have had a gift from Moja.

One of the engineers who came that afternoon was the sort of man who reads *Scientific American*, has a radio transmitter in his backyard, and might even at one time have put together his own X-ray machine for the fun of it. He alone was confident that anything could be done with the heap of chrome and enamel.

'The thing to do is to give me a part, any part,' he told

them. 'Then you guys bring me a part at a time till we find the one that goes with it. Then we repeat the process. Slow and sure. Like the German guys who put it together.'

The process appealed to David. It made for long enjoyment of the lightly-greased, highly-polished contents of all those parcels from Moja.

So the afternoon was spent as the engineer suggested. Jela returned at one time and stood staring at a long twisted armature assembled on the floor. As well, a commando electrician had soldered leads to the machine and would, on order, connect it to the generator.

David called out to her. 'Look, Jela. It's fitting together.'

'Hunky dory,' said Jela. Perhaps she was belittling the event. Or maybe she had picked up the phrase as guaranteed grade-A English from Mayhew's orderlies. She stood still amongst the mass of metal and wiring. Behind her back Cleary grunted and shook his head in sexual anguish. An engineer salivated and spat on the floor.

The matching of parts went on till midnight. Assembled, and holding its screen before it, it looked improbably sleek in that ramshackle place.

'You can connect it now,' the engineer told the electrician.

David flinched privately, expecting an explosion. 'Cover your eyes with your hands,' he told everyone, trying to save himself theatre work.

The engineer chastised him. 'It's not going to happen, sir.'

'It mightn't even be the right voltage.'

'Yes it is. We didn't even have to use an adaptor.'

No one believed, however, in the engineer's optimism. Mayhew both covered his eyes with his right arm and protected his temples with his left.

'You're the one who ought to flick the switch, sir.'

As chairman, David approached a black switch on the flank of the machine. Instead of a sizzling and an electric bolt of fire, there was the deep hum of an operative X-ray apparatus.

He stepped behind the screen. Everyone in the room could see his chest exposed.

Someone said, 'Jesus, look at his heart going.'

Cleary sang. 'You can see what the rakia's done to a constitution that used to be once youthful!'

Regardless of the danger from radiation, David wanted to lean over that screen grinning, the way a successful farmer leans over a fence grinning, his harvest at his back.

Chapter 9 An Extra Organ

On the afternoon of Easter Sunday Pelham was working through a medications list with Jela. Jela kept silent and her eyes were red. The tubercular woman's baby – together with his plump stepmother and force-fed stepbrother – had been sent away to Italy by trawler the evening before. Today Jela's grief made her appear sullen and erotic. She had a larger aura and reminded him of some continental film actress – of Dietrich perhaps.

At his tall book-keeper's desk they worked with their heads together and when they looked up saw a short, sandy-haired officer standing in the doorway. His cap was off and under his arm. It carried a medical corps badge. He was a major. Pelham's first thought was – a tourist. He didn't stand up from his desk.

The major looked at Jela as if her presence were unfair, as if on the far side of the Adriatic he had a right not to be tempted.

'Captain Pelham?' he said. 'Ellis is my name.'

David did not stand or offer a hand to him. The man blinked, a little disquieted. He covered up with some chatter. 'Southey thinks you're Jesus Christ, you know. I've been looking forward to meeting you. Needless to say, it's my honour to be able to work with you.'

'Please come in,' David said unwelcomingly. A mad impulse told him that if this man wanted to be friends he should have turned up months ago.

'Is that all?' Jela asked. When Pelham said yes, she walked out, body stiffened by loss, in a way that showed off her buttocks. The major took her place at the desk and handed Pelham his card.

It said: Major Patrick Ellis MB, FRCS,
Consultant Orthopaedic Surgeon,
St Bartholomew's Hospital,
London.
Contributing Editor, *British Journal of Orthopaedic Surgery.*

A year ago, Pelham thought, such a pedigree would have dazzled me. He put the card aside.

'That's a striking lass,' said Ellis. 'Not your fiancée or anything?'

'No,' said David without expression.

'Do you really get shot for touching those girls?'

'I'm afraid so, yes. I've seen it happen.'

So informed, the surgeon shook his head quickly, sharply, many times. As though Jela had left the room full of gossamer and his ears were meshed in it.

'I can tell you weren't warned of my arrival. The first thing I have to do is apologize for not coming earlier to see you.'

'Do you mean you're staying?'

'The Foreign Office sent me. They thought the . . . the traffic was a little heavy for one man.'

'So you're in charge then,' Pelham said, relentless.

'I was hoping we could ignore all that ballocks about who's in charge.'

Somewhere in Pelham was a rational panic, a pulsation that confessed how much he needed the man he was now busily making an enemy of.

162

'Did they tell you we'd be invaded? And that no one takes prisoners.'

'They said the chances of invasion were diminishing somewhat.'

'Glad to hear it,' said Pelham. Secretly, he *was*. 'I imagine you've come to ask for Mayhew's orderlies back?'

Ellis waved his hand. 'Christ, no. Well perhaps we could share them, eh? And I believe you have an X-ray machine?'

'You can't have it. It's a personal gift.'

The surgeon pursed his lips and looked at the table. Then straight at David. David thought, why is he so conciliatory? Say, if two or three years ago I had had to work with a man like this, he wouldn't have been conciliatory. Any more than Lady Astor would be to the man who works the lift.

'Will you believe me,' asked Ellis, 'when I say I didn't come to take it? I came to ask, can I use it when I need to?'

'Of course, there are things I can borrow from you, sir. No doubt you're pretty well equipped.'

'You're welcome to anything I have. I can itemize it all for you. A few canisters of gauze, a few more of plaster. Some carboys of ether. A portable operating table. Last of all, a sort of surgical pannier they used to issue to the Indian Army round about 1925.'

David stared at the corner of the room, half-smiling and almost flinching in sympathy. The FRCS was starting as barehanded as he had.

'Excuse my rudeness, sir,' David said. 'Will you please have a drink with me?'

The glasses were poured. Ellis smiled broadly. A round-cheeked, blatant smile to come from a consultant surgeon of say, forty-two years.

'Did you have a good journey?' Pelham asked, making conversation.

'Sick all the way, I'm afraid.'

163

'Do you get sick every time you sail?'

'I . . . don't sail. I ought to make it clear. I don't belong in the Old-Boys' set-up. I got this job by accident. I'm a scholarship boy, really. No Eton or Harrow in me. Felt a bit out of it in Mola. Of course, very rich living. Girl called Caroline was kind. Do you know her? But I was a bit out of it with the other officers. They have a quite famous officer there, waiting to be parachuted into Yugoslavia. Famous novelist. Evelyn Waugh. Very snooty. Hard man to deal with. Quick wit. Couldn't understand half his allusions.'

'They're a bit ridiculous, that crowd.'

'My father,' said Ellis, 'was a tenant farmer.'

David called in his staff. They discussed ways to provide Ellis with necessities. They spoke of the Dakota, Cleary's shoplifting on the night wharves of the port of Mus. You could see the little man grow happier as they talked.

That night they ate and talked late, and before they slept a trawler brought in a young woman with a bayonet wound in her right side. It was one of those weeks-old injuries the Yugoslavs dragged round the mountains with them and then down to the coast. A dirty, crusty, red and jagged hole.

They examined the wound together.

'Ask her how long ago it happened,' Pelham told Jela.

Jela asked but the woman was fevered and did not answer. Jela asked again. The woman replied.

'She says the second Tuesday of Lent.'

Somehow Pelham was pleased to see the honest shock on Ellis's face. 'That's five weeks,' David murmured, for the new man's information.

'But,' Ellis said softly, 'that wound *must* have perforated the colon. It *must* have caused a sinus. And it *must* have induced peritonitis.'

Pelham told Jela, 'Ask her how she treated it?'

Again a question in Serbo-Croat and an answer.

'She says she washed it as often as she could with rakia.'

At the concept of the molten liquor in that wound, Pelham's genitals contracted. The woman on the table blinked and was mute. Ellis began wiping sweat from his palms with a khaki handkerchief.

'Jela,' said Pelham, 'give this lady a quarter grain of morphia.'

Going back to the mess, he and Ellis stared about them into the dark. Both of them were afraid of the German imminence, each of them knew the other sensed his fear. They weren't spiritually equipped to face bayonets, the way the girl was they'd just left. Yet their shared fear was a bond.

'David,' said Ellis. 'When you operate on her, may I observe?'

'Well of course.'

'Do you know how lucky you are? To work on such wounds? At your age?'

'Yes, it's all delightful.'

Yet saying it, David laughed. He was catching from Ellis the habit of straightforward laughter.

Soon Pelham knew why Ellis had been sent. There was a rumour that head-on assaults were planned for later in the month. An assault on Korčula probably. And on Mljet.

Even the uninformed could guess that something of greater stature than a raid was intended. Partisan staff colonels visited Mus and Vis. RAF Intelligence officers were flown in to confer with Southey and the commissars, and the former Royal Yugoslav Navy officer who was now Tito's Admiral sailed into Mus at night to meet with Hugo Peake.

Whatever was planned, its purpose was to purge the enemy of his intentions against Vis and Mus.

Pelham and Ellis knew a great test was coming. They set up a second operating table in the theatre and spent the evening drinking and becoming close friends. They knew friendship would help them when the casualties arrived.

It was a mystery to Pelham why Ellis was there at all.

'You must have volunteered.'

'I was invited to. By someone in the Foreign Office.'

'And you did. If I was a consultant at Barts, I'd never do a thing like that.'

'No.' Ellis examined his hands as he often did. It was a temperamental thing and had nothing to do with his being a surgeon. 'Well, I wouldn't have thought I'd do it either. I was all right till I turned forty. I even thought I was a clever fellow. Then the day I turned . . . you see, I'd been carrying that date round with me since childhood as the date when everything starts ending. Well, suddenly I didn't know how to face growing old with the one woman and becoming more and more detached and wealthy. The old problem of dying before you've lived . . .'

'You shouldn't be telling me this. You're too senior to be telling me this.'

'Oh it's the *prošek*, you see. Actually, that's a rotten thing to say about growing old with the same woman. She's a nice girl. It isn't any frantic fusion of souls and bodies but that sort of thing never happens in Britain, if anywhere else. It's a . . . a decent . . . a *good* marriage.'

'You shouldn't be telling me about your marriage,' said Pelham a little drunkenly but still agog.

'The war saved me. If it hadn't been for the war I would have run away with a twenty-three-year-old nurse or had an affair with a Guardsman, though I can't imagine that. You see, I wanted to get close to my patients . . . I wanted to see them in a . . . in a more vivid light somehow.'

'You've come to the right place,' said Pelham.

'I wanted to *really* live.'

'You've come to the wrong place, you stupid bastard.'

One night late in the month a flotilla of partisan trawlers, flanked by Hugo Peake's fast and armoured patrol boats, eased up against the coast of Mljet.

It was a thin island, south of Korčula, famed for adders. Landing in the dark, the partisans found the road that runs down the low spine of the island. At first light, the air force strafed the main towns for them.

British officers who landed in Mljet for liaison described the sort of battle drunkenness, the tribal hypnosis that came over the partisans. They sang and strutted in the manner of Zulus. To back their hysteria, they had captured Italian artillery and trained gunners. When they attacked the fortifications of such towns as Polače, Blato, Babino, Sovra, it seemed they did not believe in the fire their enemy threw on them. There was no pausing, there was no taking cover, there was no sheltering in hollows in the earth. In two days, they obliterated the island's garrison, taking prisoners only temporarily, to ask them questions.

Within a day a like assault was made on Korčula. The fortified towns in the west of the island – though not the ports that faced the mainland – fell bitterly to the same lunatic methods.

The partisans left Korčula after two days.

On Mus, David and Ellis got a telephone call from Hugo Peake. More than two hundred wounded partisans had been unloaded on the docks of the port of Mus, haemorrhaging, muttering, under stars they could not focus on. Ellis wanted to operate in the same theatre as Pelham. David knew that he could weather the days of cutting if Ellis, the father-surgeon, was in the same room.

That night, and for four more nights, the wounded were brought up from the port of Mus to Momoulje by ill-sprung trucks. The first night, there were so many that they were put down on litters in the street. Ellis and David stepped amongst them, tagging the ones with the worst wounds.

They all smelt very bad, as if a sort of fermentation had started in all those open wounds. There was also a dizzying stink of excrement. You saw soon that the wounds were dirty. The wounded had been carried from the place where the bullets stopped them down to the beaches. Then there was the loading aboard a trawler. In the holds of the partisan trawler there was no light and no water. Only a bucket for those who were able to use it. At Mus they suffered rough transfer from the hold to the dock. Then to the dusty trays of lorries. When you saw such wounds under the sizzling light of a Tilley lamp, you understood once more how hard a thing it is to destroy a human.

In a weird excess of military devotion, most of the damaged partisans retained their rifles or sub-machine guns. It was too hard for the orderlies to take the weapons away from those who were at all conscious. Something atavistic in the Yugoslavs clung to the stock and barrel with manic strength. Sometimes, their wounds gaped from the effort of retaining their guns.

At each new shipment, they operated first on serious cases and women with chest or stomach wounds. The wide-eyed women in their twenties and early thirties who bore arms in the partisan forces. Many of them had come to David in the past, suffering from a failure of their menstrual pattern. Now, holed in chest or stomach or both, they were carried to the theatre by big Peko, the Yugoslav orderly. From him they had the first and last male tenderness they were likely to get on Mus.

A routine set in. The surgical teams each had a ten-minute meal break three times a day. They consumed slab-bread and cheese in one of the storerooms. They stood because there were wounded on the floor. In the same brief time they used the latrines as well.

Sometime during the following day, Ellis called across the

theatre. 'David, we'd better eat some benzedrine. You too, Sergeant Fielding.'

'No thanks,' Fielding said. 'Later.'

Ellis yawned, 'I'll eat your share.'

When Pelham took the pills half an hour later, standing dazed, with bread in his hand for which he had no appetite, he cursed their bitterness. Now he would not want to sleep till dawn, he would work in an unreal elation, becoming less sure and stable as he worked.

The Slavophile, Fielding, devoured his meal efficiently and relished the hot tea. He should have been the surgeon, thought Pelham. And I the schoolteacher with those long summer holidays.

By the end of the second night they had run out of sterile instruments. All the orderlies were giving post-operative care, holding saline drips or plasma, tending pulses. There was no one left to do the sterilizing for the theatre teams. All the receptacles in the theatre overflowed with bloodied swabs. Fielding brought in Magda and Jovan to wash the room. Peko carried the swabs away to a place where they could be burnt. Some of Mayhew's men were ordered in to sterilize the mackintosh and instruments.

Stumbling through the wards towards a brief pause in the open air, Pelham and Ellis saw, still waiting to be treated, other partisans. They were surprisingly quiet. Their wounds, in most other wars, would have caused feelings of urgency in a surgeon. Many of them would not see David or Ellis for another day. In the meantime their injuries waited, dusted with sulpha powder and covered with gauze dressings. Now and then, throughout the day, the waiting patients would have their pulses taken. Only if they began to die would they be given plasma.

'You wanted to get close to patients, Dr Ellis. This, I take it, is close enough?'

Ellis spoke with a strange, half-drunken insistence. 'It's seven o'clock. You'll sleep for two hours, then me.'

Pelham took his rest on a stained stretcher in the lobby. At nine o'clock Fielding woke him, kept remorselessly rousing him. An hour later, before Ellis had half finished his allotted sleep, Hugo Peake telephoned again. He seemed apologetic; he promised them navy rum, a whole puncheon. But he was sorry to say trawlers with 'somewhat more than one hundred poor wretches' had entered the port of Mus. There were more women amongst them.

During that day a thin girl was carried to the table by Peko. The pockets of her army coat were full of grenades. Many more were latched to her jacket by their pins. She was strangely over-armed for a lady returning from battle on Mljet. It was likely she wore Mills bombs as talismen and charms.

Unbuttoning her jacket, an orderly dropped one of these grenades on the floor. There was a crisp metallic click and everyone looked at their feet. David saw the thing roll, rest against a leg of the table. Fielding, Jela and David also saw at once that too much of its pin was exposed. Only a few centimetres of the shaft was still in place, barely preventing the plunger from moving and destroying the theatre.

Jela stood back stiffly, waiting for the terrible fragments in her white body.

'Jesus,' the orderly said. 'What do you want me to do?'

'Get it out,' Fielding told him.

But the orderly seemed to resent orders from Fielding. 'All right for you,' he said.

At Ellis's table they didn't even seem to notice that the theatre was about to explode.

Pelham buffeted the man with his shoulder. 'Get it out!'

'Yes, sir.'

He went. They waited to hear it explode in the wards or at the front door. They heard nothing. Two minutes later the orderly came back. He looked radiant. 'They tell me the pin has to be entirely removed, sir,' he muttered.

At the head of the table, by the pentothal, Jela baffled all their expectations with a raucous laugh.

Wounds. Few of them neat. Shell-fragment wounds, wounds from automatic fire. Every time, you went ahead in more or less the same way. Cut and wait for the swab. Probe and cut and wait for the swab. Calling 'Swab!' if it were late. Hoping instruments would be late so that you might have the sweet luxury of an irritable word. Cut and clamp and probe and find the broadside of shell fragment sunk into some organ. Muttering 'Clamp! Clamp!' unfairly as the arteries geysered a second before you could apply the clamp that was already in your hand. Proceeding like a bored engine-driver. Repairing a colon, removing an eye, taking a bullet from the base of the cerebellum or sealing off its jagged course through bladder or uterus or rectum – it became all one to you. A process-worker, you did not even think of the organs by name.

There were periods when for an hour at a time he forgot Moja was gone and, seeing Jela's hands at work, presumed they were Moja's. The illusion worried him. Then – it must have been three or four – just when the night seemed to have made up its mind to last forever, he went blind. A great speckled darkness came between Pelham and the wound he worked on.

'Aah!' he cried. He felt a hand on his arm. It was Fielding's.

'The lights have blown, sir.'

'Get some bloody electricians!' Ellis was calling.

Pelham had forgotten the presence of Ellis and was pleased to have the father-surgeon near him in the dark. By dawn, Pelham thought, I'll have become a child totally. I won't be able to do anything, no matter what sympathetic presences surround me.

Soon Fielding had a lantern lit. Cleary apologized loudly

through the door. 'Doctor and doctor,' he called. 'It's that bloody governor. The motor's run mad.'

The anaesthetists kept their patients etherized while Cleary found four bulbs. Three he rigged in the operating theatre. The fourth was fixed to the generator. He sat all night, controlling the throttle with a spanner. Every time the lamp wired to the generator flared or flickered, he modulated the current. Magda brought him wine, fed him soup. He loved this: a little fuss, and for himself and his spanner to be indispensable. In the theatres, the lights surged and diminished, surged again.

He became incoherent in the small hours of the third night. It shouldn't have happened. He had had four hours sleep the afternoon before.

He was examining a man of fifty whose hip had been fragmented. David asked questions, Jela translated.

He remembered feeling peevish about the time she took to explain the question, about the expansive way the partisan answered. She turned to him with an answer. He fainted before the word left her mouth. He heard later that the partisan had laughed for five minutes at the sight. A doctor fainting.

When he woke, he saw Ellis and another officer sitting on chairs by his bed. 'Before you ask,' said Ellis, 'it's mid-morning of a new day.' He could hear the jangling of the piano Moja had requisitioned. Someone was playing out of key in the downstairs room. It sounded like a scoring for delirium.

'Who are you?' David asked the officer he did not know.

'My name's Colman.' There were brigadier's tabs on his battle-dress. 'I got here last night. To inspect all this. As one might say, holy cow!'

'Are you a doctor?'

'Yes. I think, son, you've done enough.'

'You mean I can go back to Italy?'

'Yes. A soft job in Italy for you. At least, that's what I'll recommend to the Foreign Office. They say they'll be guided by my recommendation. You should be out in a fortnight. Does that please you?'

'Yes.'

At this curtness the man chuckled. He crossed to the window and looked out, as if the yards and square were still full of the mutilated. Perhaps they were, David thought, perhaps there'd been another boatload.

'I never thought I'd see anything like this. I've read descriptions of the Crimea . . .'

Before going out, the brigadier stood by Pelham's bed and put a hand on his hand. David thought, it's very well for you, friend. In two days you'll be back in the Imperiale, telling some soft woman from Littlehampton about the exceptional sights you saw.

Ellis remained behind. 'I'm a bloody good surgeon. One of the best. It wouldn't become me to pretend otherwise. I must say, mate, you're pretty good too. If ever I can do anything to help your career . . .'

David felt too leached out to consider that artificial concept *career*. 'Damn my career,' he said.

He thought, I am becoming a gruffer man, a man for expletives. It isn't like me.

When he walked out that afternoon, he saw the crushed violets around the hospital grounds where the wounded had been laid. The air was full of blow-flies. He felt tenuous. There was muttering from the wards. All the wounded seemed to be talking softly to themselves or to orderlies.

Inside the door, on a pallet on the floor, tended by a commando with a sub-machine gun, lay a German sergeant. His arm was in a sling. When he saw David, he uttered the German word for 'amputate' and made a cutting motion.

The commando told David: the man belonged to Brigadier

Southey. He had been taken on Korčula by a British officer. They had got him to answer their questions by promising immunity. Hence the guard on him.

Pelham turned to the sergeant. He was younger than it would first have appeared. He looked Pelham straight in the eyes.

'Why amputate? *Pourquoi?*' David too made the pantomime of limb-chopping.

The sergeant said nothing. Instead, with his one good hand, he pointed to the wounded all around him. What he was saying was: I would feel safer with a greater wound. With a wound like theirs.

'There's nothing I can do. Sorry.'

He left the man and began his tour of the partisans. An hour later, from the far side of the ward he saw Jela approach the sergeant with a hypodermic. David could see her talk to the German in a conversational way. She was said to be fluent in German. Poker-faced, she moved his sleeve back. The drowsy commando did not so much as look at her. Idly, the sergeant glanced at the needle. He saw nothing wrong with it.

Yards away, David did. The syringe was quite empty.

'Jela,' he roared. The yell cut through the uneasy fevers of the place. It started a spate of calling and muttering amongst the delirious. Jela alone seemed not to hear and worked at her leisure. She squeezed the man's arm, trying to raise the artery on the inside of his elbow. If she could shoot a burst of air into it, the sergeant would die within an hour or two of a fat lump of air in the lung. Air embolism they called it. It was as fatal as a vast clot of blood.

The sergeant, however, had heard Pelham yell, now began fighting her. He even tried to raise his right arm in its splints against her. Jela changed her grip on the syringe. It became a knife. She had his abdomen in mind.

The commando moved in and trampled on her. The metal

stock of his carbine resounded against her jaw. She knelt, rocking on her haunches. Her hand, four inches from her jaw, indicated with spread fingers the extent to which she expected the injury to swell.

The commando was telling her, 'Sorry, miss. I didn't mean that.'

There was already a long bruise. Coming from behind, David lifted her by the elbow and hustled her into the X-ray room.

'What were you doing?'

'You know, doctor.' She scarcely moved her lips, this polyglot girl.

'Why?'

He saw the quick colour in her cheeks. It was superb skin there. What's the matter with you? he asked himself. Her bruises and her red cheeks are getting at you.

She said, 'You want to hear some dreadful story. That I was married. That my husband was taken, one amongst a hundred. That all the families had to watch. That's the sort of story you want to hear.'

'Is it the truth?'

She began cursing him in Serbo-Croat and beating at his face. He thought, I have to have her. But when he took her in his arms, her fists crunched up against his chest, he knew that it was all impossible here. This was the room where Moja's substitute presence stood – the great machine.

After a few seconds of sexual guilt, he understood that Moja, ironic Continental, could have anticipated just this weakness in him. Mrs Javich had arranged for this quiet, smooth, furious girl to come to Mus and supplant her. If he touched Jela, it was all according to the Javich plan.

Therefore he stepped back from her. Her arms did not easily open to let him do it. After her attempted murder and her blow to the jaw, she wanted to be held.

'They don't deserve,' she said, 'the air they breathe.'

David slapped his thigh. 'I will get you into great trouble if you do it again. Now show me your jaw.'

He felt the fine-textured upper jaw for fractures, found none, and painted the bruise with tincture.

On his way out the door in the evening, Pelham was again stopped by the sergeant. The old-young face looked whimsical. It was amused by the odds against its survival.

'*Herr Doktor, ab schneiden?*' Again the cutting motion with the left hand.

He looked like a Teutonic understudy to Callaghan, the Australian flyer. David could not help liking him. An orderly was called and a broom cupboard was found for him. For he would be safer out of sight.

Yet in the morning he was gone, even from the broom closet. David found the commando guard drinking cocoa in the mess. He looked dispirited but made no apologies.

'You let him go?'

'He vanished, sir. While I was having breakfast. Maybe he got taken. The brigadier doesn't want him any more. So I'm not going hunting for him.'

For part of that morning, David wandered the island, storming at commissars. One of them was from Tito's staff and had an interpreter, who said that the doctor was under the control of the partisan movement, and not the partisan movement under the control of the doctor. However, no one had been authorized to remove *that* patient. Perhaps he had escaped.

David challenged the commissar. 'Then find him.'

To Pelham's surprise, the commissar took notice of this order. Partisan search squads were sent out, some to the hills girdling the plateau, others to the beaches and inlets. That day a thin wind was blowing out of Austria. It whined through the gap-toothed rim of the plateau of Mus. A great wind would follow it. The searchers had only the afternoon. Not that David believed they had anything to find.

Before dusk, they came across the man. He lay above the sea on the eastern side of the mountain, facing Korčula, that poor substitute for home and safety. He was lying flat in a rare clump of furze. They took the trouble to carry him back, though he was nearly dead.

When the man was laid on the table, David saw three narrow wounds in the area of the heart. Though the sergeant was conscious, his eyes kept rolling. The heart had not been punctured, but a lung. The result was the sergeant was drowning slowly of oedema of the lung.

Reaching his conclusions, David turned on the leader of the search party. Fury was one of the languages partisans understood. The officer made a humble speech. With motions of his hand he indicated what he was saying: the sergeant had inflicted the wounds on himself.

David would not believe him. He thought, if they can shoot their own sisters, if they will harry Suza and execute Callaghan's girl, they will certainly inflict chest wounds on a sergeant in the Jaeger Division.

Before he could say so, the partisan officer opened his hand. Against the palm were a pair of long surgical scissors, soiled with blood. They were the hospital's.

David gave orders for an operation and sent an orderly to fetch Ellis. For some reason he felt a personal urgency to save the German. Before anything was ready, the patient had a seizure. The eyes rolled up. The lips growled, the throat made a few disordered ticking noises. Then nothing. The sergeant had delivered himself from the commissars.

At the moment of the death David Pelham's vision fogged, as if he were in danger of leaving with the young man.

When it came clear again, he found himself the pacifist

he was to be for the rest of his life. In his bloodstream were two simple propositions: that the savagery of the Germans did not excuse the savagery of the partisans: that the savagery of the partisans did not excuse the savagery of the Germans. That the masters of the ideologies, even the bland ideology of democracy, were blood-crazed. That at the core of their political fervour, there stood a desire to punish with death anyone who hankered for other systems than those approved.

These are not novel ideas. They run in and out of the minds of many people in peace and war. But now they were implanted like an extra organ in Pelham's gut. They would lead him many times on anti-Bomb marches to Aldermaston. They would encourage him to join societies which his colleagues and his women would always consider beneath him.

In the first seconds after the sergeant died, Pelham thought, thank Christ I'm not a fighting soldier. I would be forced to become a conscientious objector from within the Forces. They have a special prison in the Midlands for people who do that. The guards are all sixteen stone and wear studs in their boots. Many times a day they walk over you and, at least once a day, bruise a rib.

Chapter 10 Mental Balance

The Yugoslavs remained as remote from David's understanding as Japanese. Like the Japanese they had a code of bravado. Their tolerance of pain also had an Asian quality. The great stint of operations after Korčula and Mljet was over. For days later, however, partisans came to the hospital and mutely presented wounds they had doctored themselves. They rolled up their trousers, took off their shirts and added something of their own to the pervasive stink of ill-healing and gangrene.

'What did he use to get the mortar fragment out?' Pelham would ask Jela.

And Jela would ask the patient and reply. 'He says *his knife.*'

They all wanted to be well for May Day, for on May Day there would be feasting on goats and cattle.

In fact the partisan flag, a red star trimmed with gold on a field of red, white and blue, hung from every tent pole and window by April 29th. At noon the next day the drinking had begun. Only a few companies of partisans were exempt from the socialist duty of drunkenness.

Ellis had arranged a party for the eve of May Day. No commandos came. No sailors. That night they were all standing to in case of a fascist demonstration – Ustachi or German – from the mainland or the large islands. Therefore a dozen commissars were the core of the party.

Tonight the commissars were gay fellows; they wanted to

kiss David and Ellis all the time, and tickle Jela under her fine-drawn chin. One had brought bagpipes; another a tamburica, a sort of banjo. They danced circular dances, the chain kolo, the linjo. Everyone in the circle was aware that Jela was performing amongst them and might have asked her to dance a solo. Except that, seeing her dance, none of them could have gone to their beds consoled.

Ellis fed the girl gin from a bottle specially set aside. He drank very little himself. Neither did David who, tired by his months on Mus, feared he might go the way Lawrence had. Just the same his mind played mutinously with the idea of getting drunk. Since he believed he could not do any more long sessions at the operating table, he wondered why he shouldn't take adequate liquor.

Like parsons or bluestockings, the two doctors watched the dancing together. David felt peevish at Ellis's chatter. 'Look at that girl, eh? Look at her. I would risk a bullet, I really would.'

'Do you think it would be worth it?'

'You know what happened to me. Had a nurse to celebrate my finals. I suppose nurses are pretty canny creatures all round. Half of them pick up husbands the night the results come out. I was married inside a year. Practically a virgin. Daughter of fourteen now. I mean I shouldn't talk like this. Perfect companionship with the wife.' It was the second time he had sent long-distance apologies to his wife. 'But things a little lean on the physical side. That girl, that Jela . . .'

David fought an urge to tell the man that Jela was a gift from Moja. Like the X-ray machine.

The longing left the eyes of Ellis and he remembered business. He said, 'Today I had a long radio message from Brigadier Colman. The Foreign Office and the Medical Corps are appalled by his report. They mean to ship two field hospitals across the Adriatic. One to Vis, one here.'

'When?'

'When they can.'

'I see.' David stood up. His glass, with its smear of gin in the bottom, somehow annoyed him. I'm going to get a tumblerful he told himself. 'I'll be surprised,' he said, 'if you see them before August.'

Ellis looked at the floor and compressed his lips. Well, David thought, he gave me a little confection of news, and I trampled on it. 'Sorry, Ellis. I'm a rude bastard.'

'Don't flatter yourself. You're exhausted.'

Six months in Yugoslavia, and all used up! 'Did Colman mention me?'

'No. But he's an honest man. I'm sure his promise stands.'

'Very well.' He turned to seek out Jela and the gin bottle. He could feel the floor shuddering under his feet with the impact of commissars' ammunition boots.

'Wait, David. There's another thing. And it's no use getting distressed about it or trying to do anything. Because nothing can be done.'

'I don't understand you.'

'The fact is this. They have a German captain. The partisans. They've saved him up from Korčula. Tomorrow, in honour of Lenin and Tito, they're going to hang him publicly over at the commissars' camp.'

Pelham stared at the men in the mess. He saw the teeth, the brutish nostrils. He thought, they're beasts and I'm caged with them. He tried to wrest the bagpipes out from beneath a commissar's armpit.

He yelled, 'Stop dancing. Stop dancing and get out!'

A few of them did stop dancing. Most did not hear him.

'You're all bloody savages!'

Ellis soothed him. 'Come on, David.'

'Do they think anyone wants to live in the society they're making? Or in Stalin's society? Or even in bloody Churchill's?'

Ellis had him by the shoulders, a good hold. Across the room the commissars still danced. They were making a racket in celebration. His hysteria hadn't dented them.

Ellis led him out of the room and into the kitchen. Yugoslavs stirred and shifted their legs to let them past.

'You're not going to sedate me,' he kept telling Ellis. 'I've got my eye out for that.'

'I'm not going to sedate you, David, my boy. Let's drink some slivovitz together.'

After two glasses though, David fell asleep. Ellis had somehow managed to get a dose into the liquor. After all, he had twelve years more practice at the business of medicine than Pelham had.

As his vision began to slip from him, David remembered Jela's face, eyes bruised and accusing, fixed on him as he left the party.

In a way his performance was all wasted anguish. Already the partisans, dancing in a chain as the commissars did downstairs, had gone to mock the condemned man in his cage. They had opened his door, and invited him out to a rehearsal. When he was out, they kicked him to death. Pulped, he was brought to Ellis in the small hours. Ellis declared him dead.

On May Day they would bury him satirically. Only after they had let dogs and livestock chew on his meat.

Pelham woke feeling lighter than the blanket that held him to the bed. Without it, his knees might float away like balloons. Waking, he put his limbs into his clothes. He could feel the weight of the cloth. He thought, where do I have to go except the hospital?

So he went and, walking into the front ward, he saw Cleary lying in bed. Cleary's upper body was bare except for a system of bandaging round the shoulder and chest. Well, thought Pelham, I'm through the looking-glass. What next?

'Hullo, Charlie.'

Cleary had the chastised look David had seen on his face in the perilous days of Suza's pregnancy.

He said, 'I know I've got no right to ask, sir. But if you could tell the brigadier you need me here, I'll be your servant forever. You must admit, sir, I've been useful with the generator.'

David sat on a stool. He noticed that his left foot slipped off one of the rungs. The drunk and the bar stool, he thought.

'Are you all right?'

'I am, thank God! A flesh wound in the back. But the brigadier's threatening to put me in his HQ company and make my life hell.'

Slowly, for the purposes of focusing, David blinked. 'I don't understand you. Where . . . geographically where . . . were you wounded?'

'Now I know I should have got your permission, doctor. But there we are. We're all creatures of impulse. It was Hvar, sir.'

'Hvar? The island of Hvar?'

'The port of Hvar in the island of Hvar, sir. I know it's occupied by the enemy and all. But the postmaster said it'd be all right. He'd always put on a very good spread before, I must say that, sir . . .'

'The postmaster?'

'Yes, sir. One of me friends is the telephonist over at Brigadier Southey's place. You see, he found out that there's a cable between Mus and Hvar. So he telephoned it one day idly, so to speak. For the fun of it. And the postmaster answered, and knew some English. And invited him over for a picnic.'

'A picnic. Jesus, on Hvar.' David dropped his head towards his lap and laughed painfully.

'Of course, doctor, we didn't go at first. Suspecting treachery, as one has to in this world. But my friend got information out of him, see. And when the information proved right, we thought, damn it all, why don't we borrow a trawler and go over there one night? The first time we went was January.

Very cold, but he had a goat roasting on an open pit fire. There were men and girls. It was a delight altogether. It was the same this time. Roast goat. Singing . . .'

'A picnic,' said Pelham.

'It was all home-from-home stuff. Then a woman started screaming. She must have gone for a . . . to relieve herself. I imagine she tripped over a Jaeger in the bushes. They were all round about that grove. Everyone ran mad. We sprinted for the trawler. Well, three of *us* got back. Out of the half dozen. Which is more than I thought would.'

'The postmaster . . . all those other people. They would have paid for their hospitality by now.'

'It's no use thinking about that, doctor. A man could go mad with guilt.'

'Could a man?'

Cleary frowned. 'Sir, the brigadier said we were cowards to leave before the other three came. But the truth of it is, we saw them bleeding on the ground. And we couldn't have waited . . .'

'Yes,' Pelham went on, striking his lap with his left hand. 'Yes, the postmaster will be paying for his hospitality.' He stood up. 'A goat feast,' he said contemplatively.

'Will you fix me up with the brigadier, sir?'

'Do you think I should?'

'A man's a member of a family here, sir, at the hospital. I'd be lost in an army camp.'

Cleary's good manners creaked, but in his eyes was genuine terror. His mouth moved in a comic, contrite way. Pelham could dimly see an eight-year-old Cleary there, going breathless into the confessional, whispering his sins, eyes wide, mouth contorted.

'I'm sure I can fix it up.' Pelham began to inspect the patient in the next bed. Tapping a saline bottle, he muttered, 'No one to make things right for the poor bloody postmaster!'

Cleary overheard. 'The living have rights too, sir.' This

184

opinion struck David immobile. It seemed to him to be a cunningly quoted statement of Moja's. He remembered the day she'd uttered it, the day she brought a piano into their mess and turned the place into a club. Overriding objections about what the noise might do to patients.

The memory of Mrs Javich made his body slack. He leaned against the wall with his shoulder. His legs had no strength. He scarcely heard Cleary, three yards away, asking him was he well.

There was a brilliant morning in May when the old order of medical practice, set up by Moja, Fielding, Pelham, all vanished.

Fielding brought the news to Pelham. As a fancier of Slavonic literature, the sergeant had been staying overnight in the port of Mus. His contact there was a sixty-year-old professor from Belgrade, now a partisan clerk. Some evenings, Fielding would take his translations across the island to the professor. They would drink astutely and discuss the weight of certain phrases and images. They loved the *Kosovo* so well that sometimes the dawn would take them, still arguing and refining phrases, by surprise.

In the early morning Fielding would wait around the dock for a ride back to Grevisa. On the morning the old order passed, he saw a large landing craft moored at the wharf. The dockside was heaped with freshly-landed supplies, tarpaulins slung across them. An army of orderlies worked on more unloading. Amongst the supplies staff sergeants walked frowning, clipboards in hand, ticking and annotating.

Fielding sidled up to one of the piles and lifted the edge of its tarpaulin flap. Underneath he saw great tins of barley sugar, the kind grocers keep in their back rooms and fill their display jars from. One of the cans was marked '5th Field Hospital'.

A staff sergeant came up behind Fielding. '*Imshi yallah!*'

he said. It was Arabic. He thought that Fielding was an Arab and would respond to it.

Fielding realized then, yes, I've gone native in my wool skullcap, kidskin vest, faded army trousers. The idea amused and even flattered him. He sat on a bollard in the sun and watched. Commissars came down from the plateau to argue with the field hospital's transport officer over trucks. Fielding did not intervene. The transport officer got angrier, spoke in music-hall pidgin. Fielding thought, he believes he's talking to savages. Bloody tourist!

'But doctors!' the officer roared. 'Dok-tors! *Les docteurs! Engleski. Anglais.* Hospital.' He got a phrase book from his jacket. 'Jesus. *Bolnica!*'

It seemed 5th Field Hospital knew about Ellis and Pelham and intended to subsume them.

Fielding put away his wool cap and put on his beret. He thought it would make it easier for him to get a ride. After a while he approached a quartermaster-sergeant. The man stood sparkling in Blancoed webbing on the dockside. He saw the Medical Corps badge on Fielding's cap. His chest bloated with the outrage. 'Who gave you that, George?' he asked. *George*, Fielding remembered, had been the term of address and contempt used by British troops when speaking to Arabs. 'Come on, they're not bloody Rose Day badges, you know. Where'd you get it, you black bastard?'

'Quartermaster stores in Wolverhampton,' Fielding told him. 'Where'd you get yours?'

By evening, 5th Field Hospital had created a tented village all round Ellis's house. Pelham was surprised how much he resented all that canvas. He thought, perhaps I'm territorially attached to Mus. Why? I don't know. All I really want to do is go back to Italy.

At night all the officers ate in the mess Ellis and Pelham had shared. There were silences whenever Fielding or Cleary or Mayhew came in to eat. The commanding officer was a colonel from the Indian Army. Pelham suspected that his medical competence was on the same level as Bersak's. But that, after years of peacetime dining in messes in the tropics, he had a nose for protocol.

'I see you permit other ranks to mess with the officers,' he remarked to Ellis, who was now subordinate to him.

'That's right.'

'A novel departure, I must say. I hope they appreciate it.'

'As much as we appreciate what they do for us.'

'Really?'

Two days later, Ellis took Pelham by the elbow and pulled him into one of the hospital's storerooms.

He said, 'Colonel Hughes is going to take over the mess. None of our orderlies is going to dine there any more. I'm sure they realize it's not my doing.'

David said, 'He can't do it. The mess belongs to the partisans and the Foreign Office.'

Ellis squinted. 'Be realistic, David. Another thing, he doesn't want Magda to cook any more. He has his own cooks.'

'The piano,' said David. 'The piano belongs to the partisans.'

Pelham was aware of the dangerous paranoia gushing in him.

Ellis said, 'It might be better for everyone's mental balance if you gave up the piano.'

Ellis had spoken of David as someone who had a problem of exhaustion; David himself didn't see the matter that way. In fact he had suffered a loss of faith in the race of man.

In the only way he knew, by conscious effort, Pelham set about reducing the bitterness in his brain. It was a process broken into by the quartermaster-sergeant who marched in at mid-afternoon. He too bore one of those clipboards which seemed to be main armament of 5th Field Hospital.

'I'm taking a count, sir,' he told Pelham, 'of available stores and facilities. I understand you've installed an X-ray machine.'

'Yes.'

'The colonel would like a report on it, sir. And then if your orderly sergeant would help me take an inventory of your stores . . .'

'You may certainly visit the X-ray machine. You may take notes, for what it is worth. You'll tell your commanding officer that it is the property of the 22nd Partisan Division. You can tell the colonel that they abstracted it from a German hospital piece by piece.'

'This all becomes the property of 5th Field Hospital now, sir.'

'Oh?'

'Yes. If you could lend me your orderly, sir. There's the machine. Then there's the supplies.'

Pelham spoke emphatically. His teeth mashed the words. 'Well, you see, if you wish to make an inventory for our sakes, that's well and good. But you won't find anything here that corresponds with any records kept in Italy. Our supplies are either stolen from the Yugoslav hospital in Mus. Or looted from crashed aircraft. Or supplied under suspicious conditions by American Dakota pilots. Or plundered from the enemy. They aren't appropriate for the records of an organization such as 5th Field Hospital.'

'We have to leave that question to the experts, sir.'

'It was all got at so much pain. Now I won't have it noted down by some little nancy of a quartermaster with a clipboard.'

The sergeant said very well, that he'd report Captain Pelham's attitude to the colonel. He saluted and left.

David could hear him muttering as he marched down the steps at the front of the main ward. 'Man's gone bloody troppo,' he was saying.

Pelham ran after him and called from the doorway. 'This isn't the tropics, you ignorant bastard.' He was aware of something on his arm: Jela's hand.

'Captain Pelham,' she said.

Cunning rose in him. He thought, it will benefit me if I surrender utterly to that small hand. She led him across the square to Magda's kitchen. I am trembling, he was aware. But my trembling is partly a game. Of which I ought to be ashamed.

All the way across the square she chattered at him. She was proud of the way her English had come on. 'It is shameful. You need very much a rest. Now all these other doctors are here, let them do the work.'

In the kitchen she found a slivovitz bottle. 'No,' he said, 'make me some tea please, Jela.'

He knew that half the reason for his trembling was that she was open to demands from him. If I want to, he thought, I can bury my face in the white hollow where her throat meets her shoulder.

He said, 'I shouldn't be like this.'

'Nonsense. You have had too much effort.'

After all, that ruinous surgeon Bersak had never fallen apart. Self-hate snaked through him. He laid his head against her right shoulder and breast. She accepted it. He could feel her moist mouth moving on his forehead. When he handled her breasts, the mouth instantly became wider, more impatient.

He said, 'Please Jela, take me into your bed.'

'Yes, doctor. We must take care on the stairs.'

It was hard to say which one of them handled the other's body with more urgency. Milk-white Jela both coy and avid.

He remembered that she had once tried assassinating a German sergeant. At the time he had been simple-minded enough to believe that her fury against Germans was nationalist and political. He had not understood that it was revenge for the weary abstinence her country's aggressors had forced on her.

In the end she said, 'I ought to go back to the hospital. But you must rest here, doctor. Turn your back please.'

Back on to his turned back, she dressed in a corner. She hugged him avidly goodbye. Now *her* arms clung to *him* in the manner of demands. He watched her move towards the door. Before she was there, she turned and gave a translucent smile.

'Now we will be married,' she said.

'Married?'

'I will learn all about Englishmen. And you, doctor, you must learn better Serbo-Croat.'

He felt his senses retract back into his skull, like the limbs of a threatened turtle. He thought, white and desirable as you are, I will not face the trouble of marrying you. Generous, demure, intelligent, beautiful – it is still not enough.

'In Jesus' name, Jela,' he said. 'I can't marry you.'

She did not speak for at least ten seconds. Her face seemed to wither a little, narrow down. 'Not marry me?' she asked in the end.

'No. You're very much Yugoslav. I'm very much British.' He thought, there must be thousands of fast-talking soldiers making similar speeches at this moment in Africa and Asia, Hawaii and Hackney. There is nothing special about you, you bastard, or your needs, or your trembles.

Jela said, 'But I thought . . . when, doctor, you did not use the . . .' She made shamefaced gestures, suggesting the condom he should have used. It was clear: she considered that on an island where pregnancy was a capital offence, the man who made love to you without taking precautions must mean to marry you.

'I'm sorry, Jela. I forgot about the . . .'

She gave that terrible hiss he had sometimes heard from Moja. His blood cringed. The noise reminded him of woman's ancient kinship with cats and snakes and other gods.

'You forgot?'

'Yes. I know . . . I was . . .'

'You forgot?'

Pelham thought, she'll never believe that. That a doctor forgot that lovemaking can lead to conception.

'I'm sorry. I can't marry you.'

He had hesitated before aborting Cleary's child in Suza. Now he thought, if *she* proves pregnant, I will have Ellis abort her. So much for my earlier niceties!

'I will not believe you, doctor,' Jela said slowly.

Colonel Hughes, a tall solemn man and commanding officer of 5th Field Hospital, called in Ellis and David for a discussion of their status.

'Is it true, Captain Pelham,' he said gently, 'that you called my quartermaster-sergeant a little nancy with a clipboard?'

'Very likely,' Pelham admitted, unappeasably.

'Please don't say that sort of thing to my NCOs.'

'If I'm provoked I shall.' Pelham could see Ellis biting his lip in disquiet.

The colonel closed his eyes, as if somnolence were the answer.

'Now, listen. You're said to be a talented surgeon for your age. And Major Ellis . . . it goes without saying . . . is one of the best. I am not a talented surgeon. Talent is no excuse for ignoring the military forms by which those of us not blessed with talent get by. You're still British officers, I take it. You haven't entirely gone over to Tito's rag-tag crowd?'

'Rag-tag,' said Pelham, considering the word.

'Can you talk to him, Ellis?' the colonel pleaded but did not let Ellis speak. 'Do you have records of all your surgery? Operating notes, anaesthetic notes?'

Neither of them did. David had an exercise book in which he made notes of untoward operations. He could draw on these notes whenever a similar case presented itself.

'There isn't time, sir,' said Ellis. 'I don't think you understand the conditions of our work up to now. Mine. And

Pelham's in particular.'

'Contempt,' the colonel uttered softly, naming their state of mind. 'Contempt. What do you two want? Do you want me to do penance for not getting here earlier. For not being an FRCS?'

Ellis turned to one side and lowered his head and shook it.

'From now on,' said the colonel, 'you will keep proper clinical notes which will be filed by 5th Field Hospital. You will also make returns of pharmaceuticals in hand, pharmaceuticals expended, equipment in hand. All that. Do you understand? My pharmacists and clerks will do the paper work.'

Pelham said, 'Go to hell!' He walked out of the room.

Ellis caught him up outside the mess.

'You shouldn't have taken him on like that.'

'Taking notes in the rush hour!' said Pelham.

'For Christ's sake! He'll lend us the clerks.'

'Sod his clerks,' said Pelham. 'Southey will protect us.'

Ellis groaned at his side. 'He's right. You want to punish everyone because they weren't here last year.'

'Why? Why would I want to punish anyone?' Pelham cried. But calmly, privately, he knew how exactly right Ellis was.

In the mess thereafter the colonel did not speak to them. Neither did he try to enforce his directives on them. Throwing out the colonel's seating-by-rank arrangements, they sat together at the end of the table and made friends with two young medical officers who were also out of favour.

One of them pointed out an officer further up the table. 'He's just been promoted captain for refusing to talk to you two.'

David suspected you could get over loss of faith in the race by simple therapies. He made himself dine twice a week in the mess without showing sarcasm or resentment. He reminded himself that he was no landlord on Mus. He remembered all the time that Force 147 were, very likely, at this moment choosing or briefing a nice Harrovian successor for Captain Pelham.

Meanwhile, Jela kept silent to show that she considered Pelham an abomination. Wondering at her silence, Sergeant Fielding began to frown in her direction.

Towards the end of May all these little self-assertions were swallowed up in the question of Tito's survival. German paratroopers landed in Jajce and Drvar. They wanted to find Tito, to drain him of his vital magic and expose his corpse. It was essential for them to show that the man was mere meat. For even his name, *Ti-to,* This-that, hinted at something pervasive and not quite mortal.

The rumour amongst partisans on Mus was that Tito had crept out of Drvar through a gap only yards wide. It went badly for the people of central Bosnia, for Grubich and Grubich's staff and wounded, for example, that the Marshal was not found.

Now enemy armoured columns drove in against Tito's Bosnia. Partisans fought wildly to make a path to the coast for the great man.

Knowing how much he counted with Allied Force Head-quarters, Tito radioed to Italy that from the island of Vis and Mus an immediate assault should be made on the coastal island of Brač. The Royal Air Force should co-operate. If it was all done with enough punch, enemy regiments would be diverted from Tito-hunting and would bunch round the city of Split. They might even falsely consider the assault on Brač a probe for a later invasion of Europe by way of the coast of Dalmatia.

As before Korčula, officers of high rank began to land again on Mus and hold conferences with commissars. Though the individual commando or partisan did not know that Brač was the chosen island, he understood in general what these conferences meant.

So did Pelham and Ellis.

'Soon those bastards will know what it's about,' said Ellis.

By *those bastards* he meant the officers of the Field Hospital.

In the days of preparation, a band of commissars visited Pelham's hospital. They had begun to treat him with some respect. They stood in a straight line and an interpreter spoke quietly to him, telling David that the staff general, the one who had arranged the operation against Brač, wanted Captain Pelham to go with it. The captain was to attend to the wounded on the beaches.

'Tell them I won't go,' David said to the interpreter.

'Why do you say you won't go?'

'Because one can't set up an adequate theatre on the beach. You can take orderlies and set up an aid-post. But I am not needed for that. I am needed here. That's the way it has always been done.'

'Am I to tell General Djuvenica you refuse to go?' There was an unnerving clipped sound to the interpreter's questions, as if he'd learned his English in Austria.

'Tell him it will cause *more*, not less, deaths from wounds.'

'But that is what the general hopes to test. Whether it is a better thing to have a surgeon on the beach.'

'You can tell General Djuvenica that I am the expert and I consider it folly.'

By now, David was waiting for the interpreter, Sten gun and all, to accuse him of cowardice.

'I shall tell General Djuvenica that you believe he should take thought again.'

'I'll go and tell him myself.'

'It isn't possible. He is too busy.'

'To see the surgeon of the partisans?'

'Yes. You know that, doctor. Supplies, shipping, help from the air. These are more important matters for a partisan general. *You* become important only after the bullet pierces the flesh.'

'Tell him I want to see him.'

'Good morning, doctor.'

Pelham thought, my God I can't set up shop on the sand. Working out of a surgical hamper. I don't have the nervous energy.

Yet in the afternoon Southey bustled into the hospital.

'David, I believe your eccentric Balkan masters want you to operate on the beach at Brač.'

'Yes. I refused.'

'Well don't. Go.'

'I beg your pardon.'

'Obey them.'

'It's lunacy.'

Southey got in close to him, the fierce little face uplifted.

'Do you think they wouldn't shoot you? They'd shoot anyone. Obey them.'

For some reason, once the matter was settled that way, the idea of travelling to Brač elated David. He began selecting equipment. He thought, you shouldn't feel light-hearted. You'll be days on that place. Cutting and cutting. But there was some craftiness in him too. He thought, if I do this, they can't expect anything more.

He asked Fielding, 'Will you please speak to Jela? I'll need her as anaesthetist.'

'But she can speak English . . .'

'It might be better to ask her in Yugoslav.'

He heard more about Brač in the mess. There were of course garrisons in all the seaports, but the artillery and the strong points were on the hilltops. Hillsides had been cleared to provide fields of vision for the gunners on the heights. There was wire, there were minefields. The island garrison was a unit of the 118th Jaeger. A proud legion and a brutal one.

Chapter *11* A Horror on the Isle of Brač

On the afternoon of the first day of June, David, Jela, Fielding, Mayhew and Mayhew's orderlies were all driven down to the harbour. From the hills they could see that Mus had achieved some new status as a port. Half a dozen landing craft rode there. Two destroyers were berthed by the ruins of the sardine factory. At the west end of the wharf, sailors were sunbathing on the decks of minesweepers.

Pelham said aloud, 'This may well be different.'

He meant, different from all other blood-baths. They had promised him it would be. There would be ships to take the wounded from the beaches back to Mus or even Italy. He would need to operate only on the worst wounded. It was a comfort to believe in the promises of commissars.

Around the mole a partisan fleet of caïques and schooners was moored. Pelham and his squad had a place on one of these small ships. In the dusk, Hugo Peake rode around the harbour in a power boat informing navy vessels by megaphone of the order in which they would leave the port. He was wiser than to impose an order on the partisan boats. They had their own arrangements, as mysterious as those of Bedouin.

From the schooners and from the hills there was a great noise of conflicting harmonies. The partisans were singing – wildly as drunks. They did not all sing the same song. Yet Pelham grew intoxicated, as he had the first time he heard the partisan chants. The cadences nudged you towards forgetting that at the end of the song lay the thud of steel fragments in flesh, and choking, and haemorrhage.

Now one of Hugo Peake's officers was reading a meteorological report through the loud hailer. South-west winds five to ten knots. Slight swell. Smooth seas. A wide cold front in the Atlantic. Not expected to influence conditions in the Dalmatian Coast area. None of the Yugoslavs on the schooner where Pelham stood seemed to listen or be curious as to what the foreign officer was saying. They laughed and hauled on the mizzen sheets. The barbaric singing went on.

In the stern Pelham waited by a vast clumsy tiller. He watched Jela and Fielding talking softly in Serbo-Croat and English. Fielding laughed at something. From Jela there was a shy but cunning smile. They looked well together, private amongst the confusion. For a second David wished they would speak to him, making him welcome.

'Seasick yet, Captain Pelham, doctor, sir?'

David peered up at the dock. Cleary stood there. Equipment entangled him, his carbine hung across his chest. On his back was strapped something that looked like the long tube of a Bangalore torpedo.

'We're not going till later in the evening, Captain Pelham, sir. With the fine boats we have to travel in there's no rush. As you're being seasick off Hvar, you'll see us zoom past.'

You're a tough man, thought Pelham. You mention the name of Hvar lightly, as if there were never a postmaster and a party in a clearing.

Instead of saying this, Pelham asked, 'How does the brigadier intend to use you?'

'He attached me to his own headquarters company.' Cleary made a face. 'I am to be employed as a runner. I have certain natural capacities in that direction.'

'Well, what's it like? Being a regular again?'

'On a battlefield it's all right, Doctor Pelham. It's camp life I hate above all.'

Pelham thought, you once said you feared being gut-shot? I want very much to ask you if you're afraid of it now. 'Just the same,' David said instead, 'you'll have to be very careful with yourself.'

But the songs seemed to have Cleary half-addled. Oh, he told Pelham, the good information he had from friends of the brigadier's was that there were only twelve hundred of the Jaegers on the isle of Brač. In Mus port this evening there were nearly three times that number. Vis was sending more. Artillery units as well.

So Cleary stood in the dusk, dressed in explosives, making a case that no one would be hurt except the representatives of incarnate evil. Being a veteran, he must have known himself that he was lying.

As the partisans embarked the singing became ragged and then finished. Perhaps a little reluctantly, Cleary went off down the dock. Towards the end of the dusk the twenty unreliable engines were started up. Some of Hugo Peake's boats had already left and were scouting ahead towards the west end of Korčula.

When David's schooner sailed out round the mole and turned north-east, there was enough light left to see the boats around him spread their sails. Tacking and, within seconds of each other, jibing to run before the light wind. When he saw the booms bear the mainsails across, it was the peak of his exhilaration. So too for everyone else. But the dark came down then and made them all solitary. Pelham listened to the soothing racket of wind and canvas and timbers under pressure.

He was aware of Fielding squeezing past the helmsman, looking for him.

'Sir, I thought I should talk to you about casualties? The number of likely casualties, I mean?'

Pelham snorted to show he didn't like the subject. He wanted to ask the man, why in the hell did you leave Jela's side to talk about such things? In the end he said, 'They haven't said much to me.'

'My source is a friend from Brigadier Southey's staff.'

'We'd all know nothing,' said Pelham too meanly, 'if it weren't for friends on the brigadier's staff.'

Fielding would not of course be stopped from saying uncomfortable things. 'The minefields are very extensive and well-planned. There are artillery positions sited to cover all the beaches. It wouldn't even be tried if it weren't for Tito. I . . . didn't know if anyone had made that clear to you, sir.'

'Not quite.'

He felt very sour at Fielding, at the man's sincere insistence that Pelham could go to Brač rationally aware of the dimensions of the ordeal. Pelham might have told him, I am a partisan. It will be unreason and illusion that will get me through the coming days. 'Maybe it won't be so bad,' he muttered.

Fielding remained, in silence. His presence a sort of reproach. Pelham felt the sergeant might be about to lose his temper and begin haranguing. As if he really wanted to raise a number of grievances against David, not just David's dislike for solid advice. But, 'We'll have to see,' he conceded. He turned and found his way back to the port side and Jela. David thought, he's only postponed reciting his log of contempt for me. After Brač, if there is an after-Brač, he will start to speak.

A company of partisan infantry rode on the for'ard hatches and on the deck, crammed up into the bows. Occasionally you heard laughter from them.

Earlier, while there'd still been light, Pelham had seen one of them hold up a broken-down timepiece, turn it back and forward by its strap, mocking its irrelevance. You could be sure that there was scarcely a watch between them. For a watch was a tactical item. They did not know what tactics were.

They had no faith in synchronization.

Therefore Southey had despaired of sharing complicated tactical plans with them. They took less account of the tactical realities that faced them – high explosive, enfilading fire from within fortifications – than did the dull generals of World War I. Once landed on the island of Brač, they would move in different directions, to different objectives. That would be the extent of their sophistication.

So that Fielding must be right. In a landscape of shaven hillsides, minefields, strong points, observation posts, there *would* be many partisans falling down.

David found that the palms of his hands itched. Oh Christ no trembling, he warned or begged himself. He began doing mental exercises again. It's as simple as this, he told himself. There is a queue of injured and you deal with them in turn. You clean up some and do spot work on others. Then they're shipped back to 5th Field Hospital, its bright-faced MO's, its excellent beds.

While he performed his mental therapies, they rounded the western hump of Hvar. Such a short journey from Mus to Hvar, and even shorter from Hvar to Brač. If there's a jaunty commandant on Hvar, someone like Southey, then he will punt his garrison across to Brač and catch us between the beaches and the heights. In that case, thought Pelham, I will quickly be relieved of my surgical duties. One terror cancels out the other . . .

The fleet edged in towards the broad beach on the southwest side of Brač. David could see the lamp flashes from the dark slopes behind the beach. These were guide lights held by the partisan guerrillas of Brač. Even without them, the luminous reach of sand would have been easy to find in total dark.

'They're running aground,' Fielding shouted to him.

All the flat-bottomed partisan craft were grinding into the shallows. Their own ship bumped and grated on a shelf of sand. He could hear all the partisan infantry and the crew laughing at the experience. They believed high tide would lift them off before dawn.

'Well,' David said. The enthusiasm of the word shocked even him. He found himself jumping over the gunwales, flinching a little for the unknown water. It was barely knee-deep. There was no shock to it. Warm as blood it invaded his boots.

'Give me something,' he called out. 'To carry.'

Jovan, the droll little Serbian orderly, put a canister of lint into his arms. He crunched ashore over shingles. Enemy territory, he thought. The grass grows here, too. There's no problem.

Italian artillery, manned by partisans, fussed over by British gunners, was being brought ashore from the landing craft. Commando officers hissed, 'C Company here!' 'Bring up your section, corporal!' Partisan infantry, following a few grunts and hand waves from their officers, milled inland without ceremony. Meanwhile, old Admiral Harris and a beach officer fifty years his junior supervised the piling of equipment above high water mark.

'Come on, come on,' he roared at the ratings handling cargo. 'I guarantee you against hernia. There you are.'

Somehow, in the diverse darkness, Cleary discovered Pelham. There was a black gel on Cleary's face, so that Pelham did not recognize him till he began to talk.

The message Cleary handed him read, *Pelham. There's a farm complex four hundred metres up the road to your north-east. I have already established a headquarters in the barn. You're welcome to the house. It's smaller.* Signed Southey.

Behind the beach ran a rough cart track. Cleary led them up it. Partisans going inland, being less laden than commandos, carried the stores. After a little walk, Pelham could see the farmhouse and barn. At the farmyard gate stood a placid old man and a placid old woman to greet David and the others.

With a little smile they kissed Jela, then David, then Fielding. 'We are welcome,' Jela conveyed, grudgingly, to Pelham.

'They'll have to go with us when we leave,' said Fielding. 'Otherwise . . .'

'Of course. Jela, ask the old lady if we can see the house.'

There was a fuel stove in the kitchen and a vast family table, as if the old people had once sat around it with at least a dozen children.

'Ask the old lady to keep the fire going, Jela.'

Jela said, 'It is not easy. They speak the Chakavski dialect on Brač. Not all Yugoslavs speak the same language.'

It was like an accusation of ignorance.

'I know that, Jela. Do what you can.'

He looked at the pumice-stoned table. Behind him Jela and the old lady had, in fact, no difficulty in their long conversation. In the middle, the old woman laughed.

He thought, this is the one, this is the terrible table. He knocked it with his knuckles. There were depressions in it which the old woman had made with pumice-stone. 'This will have to be washed with carbolic,' he called to one of the orderlies.

Fielding behaved as infallibly as ever. Mackintosh put down, as it should be. Sterile towels laid out. Canisters of swabs. Why do I feel tonight that it's all somehow aimed against me?

Cleary brought another message from Southey's headquarters across the farmyard. It said, *HLI will commence assault 0400 hours.*

'What is HLI?'

'Highland Light Infantry. From Vis.'

David closed his eyes for a second. 'Kilts?' In the black behind his lids, he seemed to see bloodied kilts.

'I wouldn't know, sir,' Cleary told him.

With a little time in hand, they began to robe. The old people, seeing the robes and masks, behaved as if a religious ceremony were beginning. They took chairs and sat against the wall, silent, their hands together in their laps. Occasionally, like a votary tending a sacred fire, the old lady got up and tiptoed across to fuel the stove.

For the last quarter hour before four o'clock, there was nothing to do. It was hot in the kitchen and the white walls, under the light of half a dozen Tilley lamps, dazzled you. A young officer with a tape measure and sketch-map stood in the open door and showed Pelham, as a courtesy, where the bleeding would be lain in the farmyard. Then he was gone. Occasionally Pelham would ask Fielding a question.

'They're bringing more plasma tonight?'

'Yes, sir. It's all arranged.'

At eight seconds after four o'clock the hills burst out in fire.

But the first victim did not arrive in the farmyard for another forty minutes. He was a Highlander whose age could not be guessed at. Both his legs were gone, and he'd suffered fragment wounds all over the body. One of these had blinded him. At least one eye was gone for good: you could see the bloody socket.

'Don't go up there,' he said over and over again, all the way to the table, counselling the orderlies, the surgical squad. 'Don't go up *there*!'

By five o'clock, there were a dozen frightful little battles in process on Brač. The port of Bole had been surrounded by partisans, bombed and strafed by Hurricanes. The port of Supetar on the north side was bombed. On the mountain road from Sumartin to Luca every strong point had attackers. By five-thirty all the young officer's work with the tape measure had gone to waste. The appointed parts of the farmyard filled with wounded and then the areas devoted to Brigadier Southey's transport.

Mayhew sorted them by quick rules of thumb. As many as he could he sent down to be put on the last of the pre-dawn boats back to Mus. The man with the tape measure watched and even timed him. 'Aren't you worried? About making mistakes?'

'Why?'

'I have timed you. You spend an average of thirty seconds assessing each case. The possibility of error . . .'

'A man has to get pretty philosophic about the possibility of error,' Mayhew said.

As happened in the earlier surgical marathon on Mus, David remembered the individual patients scarcely more than a man in a car factory remembers the individual crank cases he has bored. Time did not so much pass as lurch forward. Before anyone was aware it was a hot mid-morning in summer. Cleary came and stood in the doorway. He began to talk and did not seem interested whether anyone was listening. At the table, the surgical team continued working, knowing each other's movements intimately.

'I've just been up with No. 38 Commando in an attack on a strong point. Up near Nerežišće. Those bloody Jaegers have even gone to the trouble of mining the vineyards. They sat up in fortified gun emplacements. No. 38 made three assaults. In the end they got in close with grenades and flamethrowers and made it into the main bunker. But they only found the mortal remains of twenty of the sods. No. 38 lost two, three times that number.'

Pelham toyed with the idea of telling him to get out, to take his battle-weariness somewhere else. But maybe he needed to stand a while close to people he always spoke of fulsomely as 'me family'.

In fact, Cleary's equation, casualties of two or three to one, seemed to be repeated all over the island all day long. In the shade behind Southey's barn four dozen commando corpses lay, blanketed and tagged. A little way away, partisans covered with tarpaulins, nameless, plentiful.

A Horror on the Isle of Brač

And in the early afternoon, a partisan major on the heights of Nerežišće uttered a formal and ancient curse against the British Empire after Spitfires had strafed his men.

Southey sent a message round. It said that Selka and the east end of the island had virtually fallen. David wondered what the brigadier meant by *virtually*. Southey meant to move his headquarters forward. David could now have the whole farmyard, since he already seemed to be using ninety per cent of it. But, Southey warned, he was to make sure that the road to the beach was always clear.

Cleary again stopped in the door, 'Goodbye, we're going off to do some bloody ridiculous thing.'

Late in the afternoon, Southey led his own men against the main enemy strong point high on the top of the island. He wore his quiver and his bow and, before the attack, visited the forward positions of each of his companies and loosed off a few arrows, accurate or otherwise, towards the heights. By these means he seemed to indicate to his men the sacred cause they were to die for: British eccentricity. By late afternoon they took the summit and cleared their wounded from the slopes.

The Jaegers understood the meaning of this capture. It gave the partisans the highest point of the island. They were bound to counter-attack. They began the second the sun dropped down behind the hump of Hvar.

In the first counter attack, Greenway was shot. (A few days later, the Jaegers would display his body from a high wall in the port of Sumartin.) Southey, a major, Southey's batman and Private Cleary shared a foxhole. A mortar shell landed amongst them. Cleary and the major found themselves yards further up the hill, no punctures in them. But Southey, concussed by the explosion, suffered capture; his quiver and bow too. Within two weeks Lord Haw-haw would broadcast that they were on

205

display in a military museum in Vienna.

The major and Cleary seemed to have behaved with gallantry. They formed a rearguard on top of the hill. They came down the hill last of all, looking for wounded in the dark. Cleary could not understand why he was behaving so well. Why are you doing it, you lunatic bastard? he kept asking himself. Loitering about. It isn't *you*.

A mortar shell exploded behind them. Cleary felt his middle borne away. He took deep wounds in the legs, the buttocks, the bowels and kidneys. The spine was untouched. He held himself together with his hands.

Without warning he arrived on Pelham's table. Face down, his mouth crushed against a sterile towel. Parts of the large and small bowel, bloodied and mixed with excrement, bulged from a hole in his left side. He muttered, 'I know what you can do. There's that morphia stuff.'

Pelham began weeping. 'Yes, Charlie,' he said. 'Yes.'

All he could do with the wound in the side was cut the steel out, tie off the bleeding. The wound itself he left open, burying it though in sterile dressings. Then a near murderous dose of morphine was given, and Cleary put in another room to die.

Refusing to, he was shipped to Mus two nights later. At last he would be taken to Italy. The wound turned septic a few times, he suffered two pelvic ulcers. But by mid-1946 he was back milking cows again in Clare, under the tyranny of his womenfolk.

Once Southey was a prisoner, the British officers on Brač felt fatherless. A captain they knew only by sight staggered to the kitchen door and said, 'No one is to worry. We are going to get him back tonight.' But it was a dazed statement.

Now, together with assaults against impossible strong points, there were raids aimed at the liberation of Brigadier Southey. The enterprise on Brač was for one man's sake – Tito's. And within that enterprise, the commando officers became obsessed with another man – Southey.

In coming weeks they would even return to the island to look for him. Hugo Peake's gunboats raided Sumartin. Spitfire pilots flew low over the streets, looking for signs of him. But already, that first night even, the enemy had him somewhere safe.

On the morning of the second day, David stopped. With Fielding and Jela, he stumbled across the yard carrying blankets, making for the barn. On the farmyard wall sat a British officer, black gel still on his face, binoculars in his hand. 'Doctor!' he called.

He approached Pelham, offering the binoculars with his left hand.

'Look at this,' he said with a smile, pointing inland.

David noticed that he had a weird grin and kept shaking his head even when there were no flies. He seemed to be pointing to a slope where vineyards grew. David looked through the binoculars. Focus was a trouble.

'There's a company of partisan women on that hill,' the officer told him.

David could now see them. They were moving fast up through the vineyards, taking big steps. They began falling. It was all so noiseless at binocular-distance that David thought they were merely tripping on the steep earth. In fifteen seconds one in three fell down. Soon, it seemed, one in two. He did not want to see how the event ended. He gave the glasses back to the officer, who was still shrugging off imaginary flies.

'Who,' demanded the young officer, 'said that women are only good for housework?'

From the insane question Pelham stumbled to his rest in the barn. When he awoke, he found a fresh-faced little partisan doctor, blue-suited, resting in the sun in the farmyard, drinking a little white wine. He introduced himself as the doctor from Vis.

'Are you kept busy, doctor?'

'Yes,' said David. 'And you?'

'Busy!' The little man whistled and dusted the leg of his blue trousers. 'There are two of us. Yet amputations I have done. Fifty. At the very least of it.'

His hand indicated a pile of severed limbs.

David thought, Yugoslav medicine more deadly than an enemy. He said hopefully, 'As long as one leaves a good flap.'

'Flap?'

'Of skin.'

'Skin? Of course, of skin.'

David did not have the resources to argue the question further. His own hand was already into his jacket where there was a phial of benzedrine. The only thing is, he told himself, it means you keep going till you collapse. Yet again.

And let them amputate the way they want, he thought. His one ambition was to keep his own medicine straight that afternoon.

Fielding had come up to his shoulder and was making conversation. 'It may be an easy night. I can't imagine them going at it the way they did last night.'

'Maybe not. One shouldn't, however, underestimate their madness.'

Sergeant Fielding set his mouth in a peculiar way. As if Pelham was sneering at his dear Slavs.

David insisted, 'They can't . . . switch themselves off.'

Neither they could. All night the trucks growled in the farmyard, bringing the cases in.

The third morning on Brač they were visited by a runner from commando headquarters. The island was to be abandoned by three o'clock that afternoon. An hour later a partisan officer brought the same message. The wounded were to be moved to the beaches straight away.

'I must sleep,' said David. 'So must all those who didn't sleep last night.'

By the corner of the operating table, Jela began talking secretively to Fielding in Serbo-Croat. Fielding nodded and answered in the same language. Somehow their intimacy behind a wall of Slav language irritated Pelham.

'The order probably means,' Fielding said, reporting the results of his words with Jela, 'that the enemy is marshalling at Split or Makarska. They could land on Brač any time today.'

David waved his hand in Fielding's direction, dazedly. 'No . . . We have to sleep in any case.'

He staggered amongst the stretchers in the barnyard. Bluebottles bounced off his forehead, looking for wounds. Amongst the stricken Mayhew's orderlies moved with grey faces, as if they themselves had received injuries. Mayhew himself was on the beach, arguing with Yugoslavs and the eccentric rear-admiral about which boats were to carry the shattered.

While Pelham slept, the withdrawal from Brač went on under a screen of Spitfires. No enemy aircraft appeared above them. No E-boats came thrusting out from Makarska.

Newly woken, he stood again at the end of the farmyard squinting at the bay below. Men were wading towards the ships and climbing gracelessly aboard. Two fields from where he watched the artillery battery fired and, under its noise, Jela was able to come up to his side without him knowing. He found her staring, without emotion, at the ships below.

Am I supposed, he wondered, to feel responsible for the dull eyes she turns on small craft?

'Did you sleep well, Jela?'

She didn't answer.

'Just a few more hours. Can you take it?'

'Of course,' she said.

He thought she would stamp away then, but she remained. 'Doctor, you have saved many. You have done a great thing for humanity.'

'*Humanity*.'

'Don't you think humanity is worth it?'

'Yes, yes.' He dismissed the question with a few swipes of the hand. 'But there's this question, Jela. These men and women we mend. Are they so heroic that humanity is guaranteed a sunny future? Or are they so insane we're all doomed?'

Jela's face closed in even more. 'That's a speculative question,' she said ferociously. 'Why ask such questions?'

'Why not?'

'It saps all action.'

'Oh?'

There was a spittle of anger on her lips. 'No wonder the west is declining. It's because it bothers with such questions.'

'I see.'

'They say that at Kragujevac, where the enemy killed every man in the city, you'll find amongst the graves the place where German soldiers are buried who refused to fire on the innocents. They say too that there are at least a thousand German deserters fighting with Tito. Who can work out humans?'

'If the enemy himself is complicated, why don't you forgive him?'

'I can't manage it. And don't want to.'

She stamped away towards the farmhouse. Ideologically ready to operate.

A little after midday, David noticed the firing had stopped. From the battery further along the slope he could hear British officers calling orders in pidgin Yugoslav, and the whine of trucks as the guns were hauled down to the beach.

One of these officers visited the farmhouse, knocked gently on the operating-theatre door. 'We're leaving now, sir,' he said. He could have been saying goodbye to someone he'd shared a hotel table with in Bournemouth. 'There's nothing to worry about. Everything's quiet and there's a strong rearguard. I'd leave in about an hour if I were you, sir.'

But before the hour was up, they had a less genial visitor. It was one of those large partisan officers with querulous mouths. He carried a Sten gun and did not walk softly. He started jerking at them with his thumb, indicating they should go at once.

David was tying a ligature on a torn artery in a junked hip. The hip had been a sweet one, part of a partisan lady in her late twenties. Now she would never walk and, if her comrade caused too much distraction, would even bleed to death.

'Jela, tell him to get out.'

Jela began arguing with him, more and more loudly.

'Can't you bloody Jugs whisper?' David yelled.

Before beginning the argument again, Jela saw the partisan girl's eyelids flutter and shot a little more pentothal into the vein.

Beneath the debate in Serbo-Croat, David talked with Fielding. 'I have to have all the instruments. And the sterilizer. I want the drugs and the pentothal too. If you can take any-thing else, take plasma. If there's no time or room for the rest, leave it.'

'The old people?' said Fielding.

Besides fuelling the stove and serving soup and bread three times a day and twice at night, the farmer and his wife had sat silent against the wall. The enemy would put them on a spit and roast them for it.

'Tell him to get the old people on a ship,' David told Jela.

But the old people didn't prove biddable. Suturing the girl's hip, David could see them with a corner of his attention, shaking their heads.

'They won't go,' Fielding reported. 'They say they don't

want to die on a foreign island.'

'Oh sweet Christ!'

'They want to be trussed up in the yard. They want to make it look as if they didn't help us.'

A commando officer came into the kitchen and blew a whistle. Jovan and Peko went on loading the partisan girl on to a stretcher. They themselves were arguing a little about how she should be placed.

The commando said, 'All right, sir. Nothing more to do. I've cleared the farmyard.'

Out in the sunlight David shed his theatre gown. The Germans would find it abandoned there and might even agree that it was beyond laundering. As he dragged his gloves off he saw the old couple tied with rope to a sheep run beside the barn. The old man's mouth hung open. The jaw (you could bet, medically) was broken. His wife's face was badly bloodied. Pelham called to Fielding, who disrobed near him in the sunny barnyard.

'What did that bloody partisan do to them?'

'What they asked, sir.'

'I'll have him shot.'

'It's what they asked, sir. It's what they need.'

'Need? *Need?*'

'Otherwise the Jaegers won't be gentle with them.'

Pelham's team had to wade out and be lifted aboard a torpedo boat. There was a rating there serving everyone lemonade off a silver tray. The last pale men of the rear guard came down the sand. Old Admiral Harris strode in the shallows in his sea boots.

'Room for a little'un?' he called, criminally gay.

David cringed when the old man climbed aboard and winked at him.

'Captain,' the admiral called to the bridge, 'advise your

colleagues the coastline should now be searched. Wounded and latecomers. Latecomers and wounded.'

Pelham and the others climbed below. The crew's quarters were crowded with commandos and partisans, all stinking of cordite and excreta. Very few of them slept in the hot below-decks. They looked aghast, like men who have just committed a great crime.

All afternoon the small ships cruised the coast, while the admiral called from the cockpit.

'On shore! Are you there? *Engleski!*'

Expecting a shell from the heights, Fielding and Jela sat even more shoulder-to-shoulder than the scanty quarters demanded.

But nothing happened. Listening to the admiral's drawly enquiries, the shipload of veterans at last fell asleep.

Chapter 12 Zivio Pelham

That evening David was driven up from the port of Mus to Momoulje. He felt a duty to visit Ellis, and found him in the great reception marquee, haranguing two junior officers.

'Look, you work it out by pulse, colour, respiration. Is the poor bastard in an anxiety state? Does he have symptoms of internal bleeding. Have I got to do the sorting too?'

An orderly was cutting dirty bandage away from a head wound. He found a grey ooze on his hands. He turned and pushed them questioningly towards Ellis.

'It's brain, man. Brain. Get the patient ready.'

When he saw Pelham he began quivering, his hands tucked across his belly like a teddy bear's or a Mother Superior's. 'It's hopeless here, David. Their surgeon . . . what's his name? . . . Wakeham. His gastric ulcer burst. There's only me.'

'I can take some benzedrine. If you want help . . .'

'If you could do the sorting . . .'

'Did you know Rome has fallen?'

At first it sounded like a line from Shakespeare.

'I hadn't been told.'

They were like two drunks discussing world affairs.

'Well it has. For what it's worth.'

In the small hours, Ellis came into the marquee where David was working. He wore a bloodied theatre gown.

'Come with me, David,' he whispered. 'I don't know when

I'm going to lose co-ordination.'

They repaired the scrotum of a soldier with a groin wound. Ellis lasted another half dozen patients. A boy with an arm injury lay anaesthetized before him. Ellis began publicly quivering and could not stop.

'Can you take over, David?'

'No. I can't.'

'Then the others must.'

'Yes. Let them.'

The masked anaesthetist chastised them. 'The other men will do well enough. You underestimate them.'

'Do I? After those bloody tents? No, I don't.'

'Come on,' said Pelham, helping him out of the room by the elbow.

They slept amongst the bleeding in the reception tents. Still in their mauve though dirtied gowns, their breathing shallow, they could have passed for failed surgical cases, laid out in shrouds.

Covered with blankets, looked after by orderlies, they slept the whole day through. Then they moved back to their quarters and slept the whole night. The orderly who brought them tea in the morning told them that there had been a landing in France. A number of beach-heads, he said. The Second Front. Mus should never be invaded now.

'There's a big breakfast downstairs, sir.'

Pelham was downstairs first. He found Fielding eating slowly at the table.

David chatted about the ham and eggs, the marmalade, the black coffee. It was all a wonder to him. Fielding barely answered. His North Country, Fabian superiority stung Pelham, as often before.

'What's the matter, Fielding?'

'In what way, sir?'

'Your attitude. The way you answer me. What does it mean?'

'I have nothing to say to you, sir.'

'Why, for Christ's sake?'

'It wouldn't mean anything to someone like you.'

'Oh good. I live behind veils of invincible ignorance. Is that it?'

'Exactly, Captain Pelham.'

'And I suppose my ignorance extends to all aspects of the Yugoslav question.'

'Yes.'

'Sod you, Fielding.'

Fielding's anger rocked him on his feet.

'To you the Yugoslavs are unwashed savages. They don't know how to keep the score in tennis, do they sir? You show no sense, no sense at all, that they are the future and you are already a museum piece.' Fielding turned to the wall. 'I didn't mean to make a speech.'

'Go on, Fielding. Put me right. Damn you.'

'Your class, your bloody arrogant class, have oppressed half the world as well as ninety per cent of the population of the British Isles. And though you have a proper contempt for all peasants and natives, you've never been beyond dallying with native women.'

'I know what you're talking about. Jela. I don't have to defend myself.'

'Especially not to me! I mean, no one explains themselves to Marxist school teachers. My God, they ought to stuff you and put you in the British Museum.'

'Jela's not your affair.'

'I'm going to marry her. That's something more than an affair. Isn't it?'

Why do I feel jealous of the man? Pelham asked himself. Why do I want to hurt him?

'And is there any passion in it?' David asked ironically.

'Or is it merely an extension of your interest in Slavonic studies?'

Before Pelham knew it, Fielding had reached forward and, with his right fist, knocked him off his chair. Pelham lay on the floor, his own voice resounding like a bell in his skull. 'Bastard,' he said. 'Bastard.'

Fielding said without emotion, 'If the brigadier sends a guard for me, you can find me at the hospital.'

Eyes hidden in the crook of his arm, David lay still. Some dry old voice in him was telling him not to show his pain in front of the staff.

Not till Fielding was half out the door did David find his voice.

'Sergeant!'

Fielding turned but said nothing.

'I respect you. I don't give a damn either for the past I come from or the future you're moving to. Never mind. Jela has grounds for complaint. All right. I ask her forgiveness. If I don't get it I'll be very angry. That's all. There'll be no more nonsense.'

'All right.' Fielding went into the hall but Pelham hobbled after him.

'Sergeant.'

Again Fielding stopped, turned his mute face to David.

'What is happening at the hospital?'

'It is nearly all done. All the work. Except the burn cases.'

'Yes? Burn cases? I don't know of any . . .'

The brawl had adjusted Fielding's attitude to Pelham. Who could tell why? He explained the burn cases quite gently.

It was while David had been resting (Fielding said). Three sailors had been cleaning the blood off the bulk-heads of their patrol ship. They had used petrol. Someone switched on the ship's generators. In the cabin there had been a little bar-fire left on overnight. As soon as it heated up, the whole mess burnt.

The men had all had tracheotomies. They were not expected to live.

Pelham crossed his arms over his chest, hugging himself. 'Oh Jesus. Enough is enough. *Is enough . . .*'

'You should stay in bed all day, Captain Pelham.'

'Enough is enough, Fielding.'

'Yes, sir.'

'That Croatian bastard isn't worth it.'

'Tito? We shall have to wait and see, sir.'

Later in the vivid Adriatic morning, David went walking across the plateau, following the roads. In a dull sort of way he hoped to get a view of the coastal islands. He could not quite believe that their geology would not have been changed by the battle of Brač.

As he walked a jeep swept past him, then came to a halt, waiting for him. At the wheel sat a young American and by his side old Admiral Harris.

'Glad I saw you. Had a good rest? We gave them a nudge, eh? A nudge?'

The mad bird-like eyes bullied him into answering.

'It seems so, sir.'

'Glad I saw you. This France thing. Have to be there for it. No one told *me* it was on. However, wouldn't have missed Brač.'

'No, sir. It was . . . quite a jaunt.'

'Well, flying off this afternoon. With our American brothers. Look after yourself, Pelham. Onwards, driver.'

Three days passed before David went back to his hospital. He found it easy now to thank the young doctors of 5th Field Hospital who had, one way or another, looked after his rabble of wounded.

A week later he was in the wards when a dozen partisans stamped in, weapons at the port, as usual, like men arriving to hold up a bank. David prepared to rage. If they want to confiscate some poor bastard, they'll have to shoot me first this time.

Before he'd chosen his words, Tito arrived in the doorway with Kallich, the interpreter from Cleveland. There were stars on Tito's collar, the stars of a Marshal.

The mythical creature stood quietly on the premises. Everyone in the hospital grew silent and inspected his face. Peasant and subtle, earthy and solemn. And all the gusto was there of a man who loves the daylight and girls and booze, and all the portentousness of a Marxist Pope.

This figure had come to them down corridors hacked out of a solid enemy. Now it waited on their doorstep, honouring their wounds.

The wounded sat or stood up. Many of them stood to attention with tubing still in their bodies. They raised their fists. '*Zivio Tito*,' they screamed. '*Zivio Tito, Zivio Tito*.'

They had to be stopped by an order from Kallich. The Marshal spoke three sentences of Serbo-Croat to them. The voice was deep, low, extraordinarily affectionate. I suppose all great murderers have a voice like that, David thought. Napoleon, Caesar. When the Marshal had finished speaking, he raised his fist slowly into the air, drawing the fingers together in a way that showed they were all a family. The patients screamed and applauded to the point of haemorrhage.

Next the Marshal spoke of Pelham. There was more medically inadvisable applause.

Kallich translated for David. 'The Marshal says that you have shown yourself a true partisan. He says that the wounded here have saved Tito, but brave Dr Pelham has saved them.'

These compliments put a chill into David. He bowed to his patients and the Marshal. *Zivio Pelham*, they were yelling now.

Kallich said, 'The Marshal would like to see you outside. He'll talk to you in English. He doesn't do that for everyone.'

'I'm flattered.'

Pelham joined the Marshal. They strolled up and down the square. Ahead of Tito walked a screen of guards with arms at the ready. So too behind him. Kallich and a few other staff officers kept their distance.

'Doctor,' said the Marshal. 'I am on Vis from now on. You must come visit.'

'Thank you, sir. I'd like to.'

'Glad you like me. That Brigadier Southey. He never like me. He used say you take arms from Britain and orders from Russia. Damn good set-up, I used say. What you say?'

'The best of both worlds,' Pelham suggested.

'In a nutshell. Now, questions of medicine. I am sicking up all night. Kallich all upset. Last time it happens, Moja gives me little pills up the butt end.'

'Suppositories?'

'That's the one. Got any?'

'Yes, I can give you suppositories. But you ought to let Major Ellis examine you.'

'Look. It's nothing. The drinking water.' History was to prove this diagnosis correct. 'You send me the little pills up to the commissars' place.'

Then there was twenty seconds' silence. Pelham couldn't help asking the question that impended over them.

'Do you know if Moja is well?'

'She's fine. Sends her love. Dr Pelham her bee's knees.'

'Where is she?'

'Rumanian border. Waiting for our Russian brothers to come. Safe. Safe.'

'Did she . . .?' But he found he couldn't ask Tito if she had sent anything personal. A Marshal is a Marshal and not a lovers' runner.

Tito looked shrewd and was enjoying himself. He reminded Pelham of an indulgent father-in-law. You couldn't believe that this whimsical-looking man had made love a capital crime.

Tito said, 'She put a letter for you in the despatches. Bad woman! Kallich has the letter for you.'

'Thank you.'

The Marshal winked at him and shook his hand. The party moved on, leaving Pelham standing in the street. In passing, Kallich took a letter from his jacket, slapped it into Pelham's hand and ran on to get his place back, close to the Marshal.

From the edge of the village of Momoulje, Tito called to Pelham. 'Davo. When you want to come to Vis, we send the power boat. *Vroom, vroom!*'

He broke the letter open.

'Dearest Pelham,

'When I left Mus I sat on the hatch of the trawler thinking that boy believes I loved him because it was my socialist duty. He thinks, now she'll go and do her duty for the Canadian doctor.

'Don't think such thoughts. I remember you and always shall. The Canadian sometimes asks me for favours outside hospital hours but receives none on the good grounds he is not Pelham.

'If you promise to be sensible, I shall come and visit you in London. Anyhow I shall never forget my Pelham.

'We expect to see the Red Army before the end of the year. Maybe earlier. The horror will be over then.

Moja Javich.'

(The Doctor Leaves Mus, by Yugoslav poet, Milovan Aljozic. Translated by Professor F. N. Fielding.)

One fragrant night in June
we took him by force from the hospital
to his honouring feast.

221

At first he didn't want to go
thinking we had invaded his hospital
with malign intent.
He was not at ease till he saw the white tables under Mt Mushtar,
the anchovies caught by flare fishermen,
and great garnished fishes.
Until he saw the roast goat on the spit
and was given drink.
His hands at the feast were very clean
for a man who has worked a long day
wrist-deep in the gizzards of battle.
We made him drink so many toasts.
Death to the stallions of fascism, life
to all manner of odd people.
Even Chiang Kai-shek.
He was drunk before we had half finished
celebrating statesmen and generals.
Who have all, since that day, disappointed us.
And he danced with Commissar Felica, and
with Jovan, and with hefty Peko.
And with the sylph Jela who gave anaesthetics.
And with General Djuvenica
who had made up
from his own brain
a horror on the isle of Brač.
And in the quantities the doctor drank,
Fascism died over and over,
Churchill was falsely promised eternal life
(at least till 1965).
It was his happiest night on Mus.
And all the island's Gothic people
danced in and out his drunken vision.
When they put him aboard the boat for Italy
his clothes were disarranged,

Živio Pelham

he slept the good sleep of slivovitz.
Someone had written on his chest
Gotevo* 08.00.
This message was in lipstick.
Yet lipstick was not allowed on that island.

* Passed out